I0735531

When You Got Me

When You Got Me

A NOVEL

Patricia A. C.

When You Got Me by Patricia A. C.

ISBN 978-1-970072-80-8 (Paperback)
ISBN 978-1-970072-81-5 (Hardback)

This book is written to provide information and motivation to readers. Its purpose is not to render any type of psychological, legal, or professional advice of any kind. The content is the sole opinion and expression of the author, and not necessarily that of the publisher.

Copyright © 2019 by Patricia A. C.

All rights reserved. No part of this book may be reproduced, transmitted, or distributed in any form by any means, including, but not limited to, recording, photocopying, or taking screenshots of parts of the book, without prior written permission from the author or the publisher. Brief quotations for noncommercial purposes, such as book reviews, permitted by Fair Use of the U.S. Copyright Law, are allowed without written permissions, as long as such quotations do not cause damage to the book's commercial value. For permissions, write to the publisher, whose address is stated below.

Printed in the United States of America.

New Leaf Media, LLC
175 S. 3rd Street, Suite 200
Columbus, OH 43215
www.thenewleafmedia.com

ACKNOWLEDGEMENTS

I want to thank everyone at New Leaf Media who has been involved with this project, their support has been invaluable.

I also want to thank my family and friends for their kind words, their support, for being there every step of the way not just during this project but my whole life. Through my highs and my lows always fight in my corner no matter what.

I want to thank specially my wonderful husband for once again helping me bring a dream come true, I hope I make him as proud everyday of our lives as he makes me. For once again believing in my abilities and encourage me to achieve my dream of writing.

The biggest thank you to my mother who is and will always be my hero, a woman of iron, who gone through so much in her life but still fighting and still living, for letting me make mistakes, helping me get up when I fall, for put my life before hers time and time again.

Finally thank you to you the reader who took the time of your precious life to read this first part of the story that is in my mind, without you this dream could never come reality. I hope you had enjoyed every minute reading it as much as I have writing it.

CHAPTER 1

Isabel

"Shit! I got to go, Susan. I need to be on time. Otherwise, Lara will never forgive me." "Oh, is her big concert today?" Susan asked.

She knew how important this was. Susan and I have worked together since I started at Reeds Recordings two years ago. She is the one who supported and trained me as a CFO personal assistant. Mr Smith is a wonderful boss but very demanding, so he needs two PAs.

Soon it will be only me, as Susan will be promoted to PA to the CEO—well, to the new CEO, who will be Mr Reed's son. Mr Reed is a kind man. I met him only twice, but both times he was very polite. He has a kind smile, which reminds me of my grandfather. Everyone likes him. His son will take over Reeds Recordings in three months. No one has ever seen his son, so everyone is a bit on edge about this takeover.

"That's right. Can you please shut this down for me? I owe you, babe," I told Susan as I dashed around my desk and gave her a peck on her cheek.

"Wish her the best of luck for me, darling." "I will. See you tomorrow. Mwah."

I was so anxious about Lara's concert. I believe I was more nervous than she was, but I've always been like that. I get anxious about anything that has to do with my beautiful daughter. She has gone through a lot in the past four years, as I have. My husband had an accident four years, one month ago tomorrow. He was a professional tennis player, and a really good one at that. He was on his way from a tournament in Spain when his plane went missing. About fifteen days later, they found some of the plane's wreckage in the Atlantic. All the passengers were pronounced dead, including my husband, Sam. Lara was only four at the time. I was a stay-at-home mum, helping Sam's marketing team in my spare time. We were happy.

We had known each other since we were ten years old; we met at school and instantly became friends. When we were sixteen, we became more than friends, and at eighteen, we got married. He followed his dreams to become the best tennis player in the world and almost got there. At twenty-eight, he was the second-best in the world, and I was sure he would be world champion that year. But life is a bitch, and it took him away from us too soon.

I came out of the building and crossed the busy London Road. This morning I had to park my car a few roads ahead as there was an event at the company, and the car parking lot was completely packed when I arrived. When I got close to my car, a delivery van ran over a huge puddle and soaked me in dirty rainwater. "Fuck you, twat. I can't believe this. I don't have time to change. Shit, I have go in this state. I can't believe this." I was fuming.

I got in my Audi Q7, slammed the door, and braced my head against the wheel. *Just take a breath, Izzy. Everything will be okay*, I thought. *I need to speak to Lizzy. She will calm me down; shealways does.* I called her on my hands-free system.

"Izzy, how are you, babe?" Just the sound of her voice helped. Lizzy and I have been friends since we were four in reception. She was shy, and I was outspoken, so we hit it off straight away. Now we were slightly different; I become shy, and she was outspoken.

"Lizzy," I fumed, "a stupid van driver pissed me off big time."

"What's happened now? Wait, don't tell me ... you ran into a lamp post because of a van driver."

"Ha, ha, ha. No, this stupid van driver drove through a puddle, and I got soaked. You know where I am going now, right?"

"Yes, of course, Lara's concert. I'm here already."

Oh, man, I can't believe she's already there. She always gets to Lara's events before I do. "Well, keep a chair for me then."

"As usual," she said with humour in her voice. I can actually see it; she does this thing with the right side of her lip, like a little twitch. This makes me laugh. "You know I'm always running around these days. I barely have time to breathe," I said, feeling exhausted.

"Oh, how was Tuesday night? You said you would call after your date to spill, but you must have gotten home really late!"

Date? Oh shit, the date I was supposed to go on with a very handsome friend of Mark's. "Hummm, hum ... Lizzy ..." I was trying to think what to say, but she knew me too well.

"Oh, no, no, no, hell noooo. You cannot tell me you forgot about Tuesday's 8 p.m. date with that piece of ass of a man that Mark set up for you. No. Please tell me you turned up."

"Sorry, Lizzy. I was completely knackered from Lara's extra music sessions. When we got home, Lara and I were so tired we barely ate and went straight to bed. I completely ... Ouch, fuck, mother ... ouch ... ouch!" I never saw that coming. The pain in my neck and chest was really bad, like someone smashed my chest with a baseball bat and my neck had been struck from behind. What was that? I was stopped at a red light. Was I hit from behind? Oh shit, I was.

"Izzy, what's wrong?" Lizzy sounded worried. She might have heard the bang, and with my complaining, she was probably already assuming the worst. "Izzy, speak to me. You okay, babe? Please speak to me. I'm getting worried."

"Lizzy, let me call you back. I think I was hit from the back. I'll call you back." I didn't let her answer. I just ended the call from the steering wheel. *Shit, my neck hurts bad. I can't even move it.*

CHAPTER 2

Jack

I can't wait for this to be over. I filed for divorce eight months ago and moved to my new place across the riverbank. I was just starting to enjoy life again. How was it that I didn't see what Jessica was doing while I was training to be my father's successor at his company? She was actually involved with my best friend Ian's younger brother, Seth. Yes, he was younger than me by five years. He was only twenty-five. She is three years older than him. I could see his appeal to her, but he was so fucking immature, with no real objectives or a career.

"Just get rid of her today, man, and all will be better. You'll see." Ian was on my side.

Even though she cheated on me with his brother, he was a true friend.

"Yeah, I know Ian. But you know she is a fucking nightmare. She wants so much money to get out of this marriage, so she can live off it with …" I didn't finish the sentence; it was not fair to bring up his brother. Ian was too hurt by his brother, probably as hurt as I was, so it wasn't fair to bring it up.

"I know. I am so sorry, Jack. You know how upset I am and how bad I feel, mate." "Please, Ian, don't even go there. You have nothing to be sorry about. This is not your fault. You have been there for me time and time again, even gone against your brother on this. I can't thank you enough for being there, mate." Ian and I were in business school and university together and always stayed by each other. He was best man at my wedding and was still my best man.

My phone rang. My father was on the other line, so I had to terminate Ian's call. "Listen, mate, I need to go. Dad is on the other line. I'll speak to you later, okay?"

"Okay, man. Good luck, and let me know how it went," he answered and then switched off.

"Father," I answered my dad's call.

"Jack, where are you? Are you driving?" He was always opposed to me speaking on the phone while driving.

"Yes, Father, I am. I'm on my way to the last mediation session with Jessica. Hopefully, she will sign the papers today. I offered her what she wanted."

"Oh, I forgot, son." My dad sounded sad when we spoke about the divorce. He really thought this was it. So did I, but we were both completely wrong.

"It's okay. Shoot, what do you need?" I knew he needed something from me to call me at this time. He only called me before 8 p.m. if he needed something from me.

"Yes, well, you know tomorrow is a big day for both of us. I called to make sure you are going to be in on time. I need you here by 8 a.m. on the dot."

"Yes, Father, I will be." He hated when I was late. To be fair, that was very often.

"Jack, I'm serious. You need to be here by 8 a.m., no later. This is a big day, son." I could hear the desperation in his voice.

"I know, Dad. It is very important for me, too, you know. I will give everything I have to your company. I told you this before."

"Of course, my son. I believe in you. You are as passionate and intelligent as I am, even more so. I have no doubt you will bring a lot of success to *our* business." He always made sure to point out that it was not his business but ours. I felt pride when he did so.

Right then, Jessica was on the other line. "Dad, I got to go. The devil is on the other line.

I'll talk to you later, okay?"

"Jack, I mean it. Tomorrow, 8 a.m. sharp." He was now using his business voice, strong and very serious.

"Yes, sir. Will be there. Goodbye." I ended the call and took Jessica's call. "What now, Jessica?"

"Hello to you too, Jack. Where are you?" She was such a bitch, still wanting to control me in every way she could.

"I'm on my way, why? It is only 4.30, and the meeting is not until 5.10, so what's the problem?" She was clearly looking to unhinge me to see if she could get even more money.

"I was just wondering if you will be on time, as you never are. You know that if you're not on time, I will not sign this before we discuss it in detail."

"Well, isn't Mrs Corner there? She is my solicitor, so you can take up any queries you may have with her. She knows exactly what I want, and you two can chat until I arrive. Until then, please don't call me. For the love of God, just delete my number and talk with Mrs Corner. She will help you. Goodbye." I was so furious that I banged my hand on the steering wheel and my phone fell off the phone holder. I just looked at it for a second—not even that long. The next thing, I saw a four-by-four stopped at the lights in front of me. I slam on the brakes, but it was too late. I went straight into it.

"Shit." My beautiful Jaguar Sport was done, a goner for sure. "Shit, shit, shit." I jumped out and ran to the four-by-four.

I saw a lady with a hand at her neck and the other at her chest. Her short light brown hair was all over her face. She was clearly in pain and speaking to someone, probably on the phone. I opened the door. "Miss you okay? I'm so sorry. I didn't see you. I'm so sorry. Are you hurt?" she was bent over slightly and speaking to herself.

"You fucking twat. How didn't you see me stopped at a red light? Ouch, ouch, ouch."

Oh, she is feisty. Nice pair of legs too—very nice. What am I doing? I need to helpher.

She is probably seriously injured.

"Miss, please don't move. I'm calling an ambulance."

"No ambulance. I don't need an ambulance. I just need a minute. Shit. Just give me a minute." She continued swearing, and then she tried to move her neck this way and that. When she turned my way, she locked eyes with me. It was then that I saw her beautiful light brown eyes, almost golden. Her lips were slightly pulled up in a wince, full and pink. Her skin was slightly bronzed, not by the sun but by her natural skin tone. She froze, and I noticed a wedding band on the finger of her hand massaging her sore neck. I cleared my throat.

"Sorry. It was entirely my fault. My apologies, Mrs ...?"

She seemed to catch up with my question and answered a bit shyly.

"Winter. And yes, it definitely was your fault. I'm sorry for swearing at you sir. It's just ... it hurt, and I've had a shit of a day. I was running a bit behind, so it all came crashing—no pun intended." She smiled at that, and so did I. Her eyes were also smiling—I don't know how, but that's the best way I can describe them. They were shining and in slits.

"Are you sure you don't need an ambulance, Mrs Winter? At least let me take you to the hospital to get you checked out. You don't look good, you know." She gave me a look that backed me up a little.

"Thanks. That's what I need to hear—that I don't look good. Very kind indeed." Oh shit. I put my foot in it again.

"*No*, no, God, that's not what I meant, you are f ... I mean, you look nice, just ... what I meant was that you look unwell, like you just had an accident." *Why am I mumbling? I don't understand why this woman makes me feel like a small child.*

"Well, that's because I was in an accident that *you* caused."

She seems really upset, and I really hate to upset lovely women like her. Look, again with these thoughts. What is wrong with me?

She turned her eyes to me again. "Sir, could you please give me your insurance details so I can get on with my day? I really need to be somewhere, and it's getting late." She looked at her watch, and I could see her worried expression.

"Of course, Mrs Winter. My apologies. Could you please give me your email address so I can email them to you? I could do that right now." She stepped out of the four-by-four and went to the back to see the damage.

"Pffff, mine is not too bad, but yours—well, you probably won't be able to save it, it is quite a mess." She had her hands on her hips and bent slightly forward. She had a really nice ass too. She worked in an office, I could tell, by her tight black pencil skirt, her cream and red striped silk shirt, and her high heels—Jimmy Choo, if I wasn't mistaken. She looked very professional and well put together. I also noticed her clothes were splashed with dirt.

Something had happened, hence her comment that this had been a shitty day. She went into her car and brought out her card, handing it to me.

"Here is the email address to send your details to. Please do that now, if you don't mind, while I take a few photos of both our cars so I can send them to my insurance company." When she handed me her card, I just froze in place, looking at it. It couldn't be. No, it couldn't be. She works at my dad's, our company, Reeds Recordings, as a PA. Oh, she is Calvin Smith's PA, our family friend and CFO of Reeds Recordings. *That is interesting.* I typed her email onto my phone and proceeded to email her the details.

I asked her to check her inbox to make sure she got them, and she did.

"Well, I have to shoot off. Thank you for the details, and please be more careful next time. You were lucky I didn't have my little girl with me. Otherwise, I wouldn't be so kind," she said this with a little smile, but for some reason, I was sure if her little girl had been in the back, she would have been a lioness. She just had this look of fierceness to her.

"My true apologies, Mrs Winter, I will be more careful. And good luck. You have my email now, so if at any point you need any medical attention, or if you need to get in touch with me to discuss any payment for losses, please do not hesitate."

"Well, I won't need to get in touch with you, sir. I have your insurance details. But thank you. Have a good day." I noticed that she didn't ask for my name, just called me "sir". How odd.

She climbed into her four-by-four and went on her way. As I watched her go, I had a feeling of loss, a sense of sadness coming over me. It was probably the anticipation of having to deal with Jessica. Yeah, that's probably what it was.

My car wasn't drivable, so I had to call Ian. Thankfully, he was in the area. He came to collect me and dropped me at the mediation centre. He left me there so he could deal with my car. I was truly thankful for having such a great friend.

CHAPTER 3

Isabel

How strange was that man? He was very, very cute though. I have never seen such green eyes. They were like a clear, bottomless river, and his cologne was the same as Sam's, I'm sure of it, Jean Paul Gaultier—such a sexy smell. *What am I thinking? I need to get to Lara's concert and fast.* I called Lizzy on the way.

"Izzy, you okay?" her voice was urgent and worried.

"Hi, Lizzy. Yes, a bit sore but okay. It was a small crash. My car didn't have much damage, but the gentleman's was totalled." And what a gentlemen he was, with his broad shoulders and his cheeky smile. *Focus, girl, focus.*

"Oh, Izzy, I was so worried. I heard a big bang, and then you were in pain. I was going crazy here." She let a breath out, and I could feel her worry for me.

"Yes, Lizzy, I'm sorry I had to end the call like that. I needed to deal with the other driver. I am about ten minutes away, okay? See you, babe."

"See you in a bit then, and please be careful. Try not to kill yourself or someone else," she said this with a little humour this time.

"Okay, I'll try my best. Mwah." With that, I ended the call and stepped into my four-by- four. I love this car. It's one of the things I got for myself after I got the job at Reeds Recordings. I always wanted to get a Q7, but Sam never liked big cars. He used to say that four-by-fours were for mums, and he never saw me as a mum, even though I was a mum to his daughter. He always said I was his girl, a young, sexy girl who deserved to drive Audi R8 or a Mercedes SLK— "with sexy curves", as he usually put it. But I always loved big cars; they made me feel safe and powerful. It's silly, I know, but that's just how this car makes me feel, and today proved that it is safe.

I arrived at St Mary's School, where my little girl goes, and parked. The car park was quite full. There were many people today. Hopefully, Lara would not be too anxious. She is very much like her father—very cool-headed, doesn't stress over much, and always finds a joke to defuse a difficult situation. I love her more than anything in my life.

Lizzy waved at me when she spotted me at the auditorium entrance. I went and sat next to her. Thankfully the concert hadn't started yet. The lights were low, and everything was set up to start. Lara came onto the stage and sat at the piano. Everything went completelyquiet.

She started playing, and as always, I sobbed and sobbed. I was so proud of my 8-year-old little girl. She is so talented that every time she plays in concerts, I can't hold back.

Later we went home and I told Lara how proud I was of her and how wonderfully she played. My mum called once we were home. She is Portuguese, so she speaks half-English, half- Portuguese, which is quite funny. She has been in England for almost thirty-five years, and she still speaks to us mostly in Portuguese, even though we answer her mostly in English. I speak fluent Portuguese, and I taught Lara at home, but we both speak English at home. We only use Portuguese if we go out someplace and don't want people to understand, which is quite fun sometimes.

"Yes, Mama, Lara was wonderful as always. Yes, she is here. Just hang on a second. I'll put her on." I passed the phone to Lara so she could speak to her.

"*Ola, Vo*. You okay? Thank you. It was just superb, I loved it. No, no stressful at all. Yes, Vo, I will come Saturday and stay the night with you. Yes, you too, Vo. Love you. *Tchau*." She hung up with a little frown.

"She is getting very sensitive, Mummy. You think she feels alone?" My mum has lived on her own since my alcoholic father died ten years ago. She had a tough life with him. We tried for almost twenty years to help him with his addiction, but unfortunately, he couldn't leave the drink. I think all the years of verbal and at times physical abuse is now taking its toll onMum.

She is tired, and her health is not great, with diabetes among other things. I keep asking her to come and live with us, but she is as stubborn as an ox and won't move in with us. Lara sometimes spends the weekends with her, so she has a bit of company, and in a way this gives me a little time to myself, which is very rare. I usually do housework, go for my weekend evening five-mile jog, and of course, do a few jobs that can be done from home for Reeds Recordings.

I was making dinner when I heard an email notification on my phone, so I checked it out.

I was surprised to see it was from Jack, the gentleman who crashed into me earlier today. The email said,

Dear Mrs Winter,

I have called my insurers, and they have confirmed that you have made a claim for the accident we had earlier, but they have yet to receive any injury claim. I am a little worried. I know for sure you have gotten hurt and didn't claim for this. I understand that you might be a busy lady, but please consider making an injury claim. You might feel all right today, but tomorrow or sometime along the line, you might suffer, and it can affect your life. I feel terrible knowing I have caused pain and inconvenience to you or your family. You have a little girl to think about, and I don't want to cause a financial struggle to a family, so please consider this, and please make the claim. I will sleep better knowing that you and your family will be okay.

I wish you and your family all the best.

Kindest regards,

Jack J. R.

"What?" I said out loud.

"What is it, Mummy? You okay?" She looked at me from the table where she was doing her homework as I cooked.

"Oh yes, baby, everything is okay. Just something I wasn't expecting, that's all. Finish your homework, please. Dinner will be ready in fifteen minutes."

What was I to do, reply declining the claim, telling him I was financially secure, or just ignore it completely? I didn't want to be rude, but I also didn't want to tell him anything about my life. *What should I do?* I decided to reply.

> Dear sir,
>
> Thank you for your concern, but is unnecessary. My little girl and I are and will be fine. I won't be claiming injury to your insurers, as I have not sustained any injury. My neck is only slightly sore. I can move with no difficulty at all, and my chest is fine also. Please go to sleep with your conscience clear. You have done no damage other than to the vehicles, which are both covered by insurance.
>
> No more apologies are needed over this incident.
>
> I wish you well also, and please remember to be more attentive while driving next time.
>
> Kind regards,
>
> I. Winter

After I sent the email, I went to take care of dinner.

The next working day, I was twenty minutes early. Susan wasn't there yet, so I logged into my desktop and started to print Mr Smith's schedule for next week. As I went into Mr Smith's office to drop the schedule on his desk, as per usual, someone tapped me on the shoulder. I turned around with a start. Linda was there, giving me the evils.

"What do you want, Linda? Did you forget your knickers in Mr Smith's office?"

Mr Smith and Linda have been having an affair for over a year now. She is the lobby receptionist but wants my job, as it will be much easier to mess around with Mr Smith that way. Luckily, Mr Smith knows how good I am at my job and how much he needs a PA that is focused on her job, not on his pants. He is an excellent boss, but I can't understand why he would mess around with Linda when his wife is so beautiful and sophisticated. She is so elegant and always very polite when she visits. I like her a lot and wish that Mr Smith would end this thing with Linda. It's just not right, but then again, it's not my place to judge.

"No, actually, I don't wear knickers. Mr Smith likes me commando," she said with an evil grin.

"I just came to let you know it won't be long now before I take over your job. Mr Smith told me yesterday that soon I will be working as his PA." Another lie. Poor thing. She really is naive—or just plain stupid.

"Oh, did he now? Did he say it when you were holding out on him? Oh, I see. He did. Linda, let me give you a friendly advice: stop messing around with married men. Businessmen too, for that matter. They are clever, and they will say what you want to hear so they can have what they want. But be sure, if Mr Smith wanted to have you as his PA, you would have been for a while now. But in any case, if you take my job, that's fine. I am a clever woman, and I can get another job somewhere else. Don't you worry about me. Now, if you'll excuseme."

I went into Mr Smith's office and left the schedule, as usual, closed the door, and sat at my desk without another glance in Linda's direction. She just turned around and left in a hurry. She never learns. I can stand up for myself, and I always have an answer foreverything.

When Susan came in at ten to eight that morning, I told her about the accident and how fit this gentleman was, how gorgeous his eyes were, and how thoughtful he was for emailing me later that night.

"Oh, Isabel, I never heard you talking about a guy before. He must have been fit," she said with a grin.

"Yeah, he was so hot, but I will never see him again, so that's that," I said this somewhat disappointedly.

"Well, you have his email address. Why not email him inviting him out for a drink or something?"

"What? *No.* I can't do that. Besides, he got the impression that I was married. He saw my wedding band and referred to me as 'Mrs Winter'." I gave a dismissive wave of my hand.

"Seriously? Why didn't you tell him your first name? You could have, I don't know, just dropped it in that you were a widow in need of a hot man to bring your dreams to life." We both laughed at that.

"Susan, stop it. You're cheeky, you know."

With this, Mr Smith arrived and stopped at our desk.

"Ladies, good morning to both of you. Today is a big day. Mr Reed's son is being presented to the board, and he wants all the board members and their PAs to be present so he can meet everyone. He wants to get to know everyone well enough before he starts talking business, so you will both be attending the meeting. Susan, today you are going to spend a bit of time with him after the meeting to learn what tasks will he require of you. He will most likely ask you for past reports, as well as the schedules that Mr Reed kept. For this, you will have to liaise with Clara, Mr Reed's PA. She has all the information you will need, so the two of you will become very well acquainted."

"No trouble at all, sir. I am looking forward to working with both Clara and Mr Junior Reed."

"Great, then. The meeting is at 8.30am so you have about thirty minutes to get all the notes ready. Isabel, can you reschedule my 2 p.m. meeting, please? I will be busy with Mr Reed today, so I won't be able to make the 2 p.m."

"Sure thing, Mr Smith. I'll do that right away." "Thank you, ladies."

He stepped into his office.

At 8.25 a.m. we followed Mr Smith into conference room 1. Most of the attendees were already there, but Mr Reed and his son were nowhere to be seen. As we sat next to Mr Smith, Susan and I were talking about tasks that I needed to do for him this week. As she wouldn't be there to do them, I would have to perform all the tasks. It was a challenge, and I like challenges. We were so focused on our conversation, we missed the newcomers. I looked up to see those clear green eyes, like a bottomless river, focused on me. He wore a cheeky smirk on his lips.

Oh, those lips. It can't be. I must be daydreaming.

"Isabel, did you hear what I just said? Isabel?" Susan was trying to get my attention. She turned to see what I was staring at. "Isabel, stop drooling. People will notice," she whispered in my ear.

I averted my gaze but felt his eyes burning a hole in me. Shit, he was Mr Reed's son. There had to be some mistake. I wasn't supposed to see him again. I took a peek under my lashes and, yep, there he was, looking at me with that same smirk on his face.

You can do this, Izzy. You aren't going to be working with him, so you will rarely cross paths. You will be okay.

I tried to keep my attention on his father, Mr Reed. He was speaking to everyone, so I focused only on what he was saying.

CHAPTER 4

Jack

She was the first thing I saw—Mrs Winter. She was having a discussion with another woman, whom I assumed was Miss Susan Wright, her colleague and my supposed new PA. She was so focused on the discussion she was having that she didn't realize I was in the room until her eyes locked with mine. Oh, oh, those golden eyes, still very much like I remembered. God, today she was even more beautiful, well put together with her hair up in a tight bun, light makeup, her pink lips even more pink and shiny with lip gloss, and her cheeks lightly blushing, probably because she was looking at me and realized who I was. She was wearing a red fitted see- through shirt, and—oh my, oh my—does she have a nice pair.

I gave her a little smirk to let her know that I recognized her all right. She tried to look away, but not long after, I caught her looking again.

I don't know what this is. I know she is married, but the way she looks at me. God, please forgive me. I am an asshole. I don't want to do to her husband what Seth did to me. *Get a hold of yourself, man.*

"So, I'll let my son introduce himself to everyone." My father looked at me expectantly.

"Thank you. My name is Jack Junior Reed , but please call me Jack. I am here to learn and hopefully take over Reeds Recordings, with the help of my father of course. I expect everyone present to work with me with patience and understand that I bring a lot of passion and new ideas to the business. It's my goal to bring us into the modern digital world we are in. I am not saying Reeds Recordings is behind our competitors, because is not, but I want to be well ahead of everyone in this industry, so I will be bringing new concepts, and hope I will have all your support in doingso."

I kept taking glances towards Mrs Winter, but for some reason she was looking at my father a lot.

"I asked all board member PAs to be present, because I will often speak to the PAs before I speak to the board members. I need all you PAs to know that I am a very hands-on person, and I like to meet the people I deal with. Your job is invaluable for us to do our jobs properly. You have to be on the ball. I have been looking at the records, and I must say, I am very impressed in what I have seen so far. So, for your great work, thank you, and please keep it up."

I again found myself looking at Mrs Winter, and again she was looking at my father. I was starting to get a bit worried there. Was there something going on between them? I looked at my father, and he looked at me. I felt a bit relieved. I didn't know what I would do if they were staring at each other.

Stop it, Jack. Focus, man, focus.

"One last thing: I will be holding a weekly meeting with all board members and their PAs too. I want to make sure everyone is in the loop regarding the latest updates. It makes everyone's job easier if we are all at these meetings. That's it from me. Thank you for welcoming me." I looked at my father, and he had this smile on his face. I could see I was making him proud. I smiled back.

"So, everyone, now this is it. Jack will be starting officially on Monday, but from today, you will be seeing him in and out, as he will be setting up all schedules and what not to suit us both. You are all dismissed. Thank you. Oh, Mr Smith—and both Susan and Isabel—please stay behind. We need a word."

At that, Mrs Winter looked up at me with a shocked expression. She then looked at Miss Susan Wright, and they both frowned, not understanding why they were being asked to stay behind. Of course, I knew the reason.

"Calvin, how are you?" I shook his hand with a smile.

"Jack, I am thrilled you are here and ready to go. Really pleased to see you." I patted him on the back and shook the ladies' hands.

"Hello, Miss Wright and Mrs Winter."

When I shook Mrs Winter's hand, her cheeks went bright red. That only made me smile even more.

"Ms Winter," she corrected me. Wait, what? She's not married? "Oh ... my mistake."

I gave her a puzzled look, but she looked at her feet, at Miss Wright, and at everyone but me. I was very confused at this point. Then again, in her email, she only mentioned herself and her little girl, so there might not be a husband after all.

"Calvin, we wanted to talk to you. I think I have taken Susan from you, and I believe she has been with you, what, five years now? Yes, Jack and I spoke, and he doesn't feel comfortable taking Susan from you, but he is quite happy to have Isabel, who I know is also excellent at her job. However, we need to make sure you are all happy with this arrangement. Jack just thought that you might be more comfortable with this."

I looked at Ms Winter, or Isabel, as my father calls her. She had a shocked look on her beautiful face. This made me smirk yet again.

"Ladies, how do you feel about this? Susan, would it be okay if you stayed as my PA? I know you were looking forward to working with Jack, but I am used to you, and you know everything about the job. Isabel is brilliant at her job too, but she would have to do many more new tasks which would add a bit more pressure."

Susan spoke first.

"Mr Smith, thank you for your kind words. Yes, I was looking forward to working with Jack, but I am equally excited to stay and work as your PA—but only if Isabel is okay with this, of course."

She looked at Isabel with a smirk, which made Isabel frown.

"Oh, y-yes, of course, it's fine. I would like the opportunity to work with Mr Jack Reed." She blushed some more at that and finally looked up to me and smiled. She looked beautiful. Her smile brightened her face. I smiled back briefly so she wouldn't feel too embarrassed.

"So, it's all sorted then. Susan, you can go with Mr Smith, and Isabel, you can go ahead with Jack. He will go over a few things with you, and then you will meet Clara, my PA, and liaise with her for whatever Jack needs. Jack, you are in good hands now."

I agree totally. I am in good hands indeed. Let the new challenge begin.

CHAPTER 5

Isabel

I followed Jack to his new office on the fifty-fourth floor. There were so many desks and so many people working on this floor that there was a kind of buzzing sound. We went straight to the end, where there was a nice reception desk in the left corner. In the right corner was a closed office. I assumed the desk in the corner would be my station from now on.

"Isabel, welcome to your workstation. I hope is to your liking, but if you would like to decorate this space however you like, please feel free to do so. This is my office, as you can see, on the right. The door is facing your desk. Now, come inside my office, please, so we can have a chat."

I hope this is a chat about work. Oh God, let it be about work.

I walked in and was surprised by the size of Jack's office. I never thought it would be this big and, *wow*, decorated with art all over the walls. There was another door, which I assumed to be a toilet, and a huge cabinet on the far wall. I assumed that was where he kept drinks for guests. Behind his desk were floor-to-ceiling windows with the most spectacular view of London. I could make out Big Ben from here. Jack sat on the black leather sofa in the corner next to the toilet door, and I followed suit. He looked at me for what seemed like ages without speaking. I was so anxious that my hands became damp. When he spoke, I jumped slightly at the sound of his voice.

"So, Mrs Winter. Oh my, apologies, Ms Winter ..."

He was expecting me to explain. He had that cheeky smirk on his adorable face, and I felt my cheeks warm up.

"No, the apologies are mine. I just … it wasn't a good day, and you assumed I was married, so I didn't correct you. I've been a widow for the last four years." I looked down at my wedding ring and released a breath I didn't know I was holding. "Not many people know about that, so when someone assumes I'm married, I go with it, because in a way, I still am. Sorry." I was starting to get nervous. What was he thinking? Surely he was thinking, I could tell. His eyes were locked on mine, and he was frowning slightly.

"I am so sorry to hear that you lost your husband. I didn't want you to feel that you had to tell me that. If at any point you don't feel comfortable answering any questions, please do not feel as though you have to. Is it okay if I ask how he passed?"

He looked intrigued, so I thought, *What that hell? I am going to work for him, so he might as well know me a bit better. There is no harm in that, is there?*

"You probably heard of him. He was a professional tennis player, the second best in the world. When he died, he was actually on tournaments. He was returning from Spain after winning and was going to play at Wimbledon two months later, but unfortunately, he never made it."

He had that shocked look whenever I told someone who my husband was. The recognition was stamped all over his face.

"Wait a minute. You can't possibly be Sam Winter's wife." He was breathing fast. I could sense he liked Sam. I just smiled and nodded my head. "Oh God, I was probably his biggest fan. He was amazing. He would have won the world championship, I am sure of it. *Wow*, I'm stumped. I'm going to be Sam Winter's wife's boss. No way." He was beaming at me and couldn't stop moving his hands and legs. He kind of reminded me of Lara when she was extremely excited about something. It made me laugh.

"Well, yeah, you are my boss, and I hope you don't treat me any differently now that you know who I am. I'm here to learn and do my best in everything. I don't expect anything to be easy just because of who my husband was. I am my own person, and I love challenges," I said this with a serious tone. I need to be taken seriously at my job. I want to be proud of my career, to know it wasn't handed to me, because in all honesty, I don't need to work a day in my life, as Sam left me a substantial sum of money and investments, ensuring Lara and me will not want for anything in our lives. However, I hardly touch that. I want to be able to provide for us. It makes me feel useful.

"Isabel—can I call you Isabel?—I know my father likes to address his employees on a first-name basis, as he feels they are like family, not just staff. Is that okay with you?" He had a worried look, probably thinking he was offending me, even though he had already called me Isabel before. He was funny.

"Isabel is okay." I gave him a little smile to reassure him.

"Okay, Isabel, I am not an easy person to work with. I expect things to be done at a most professional level. I will be learning a lot as well for the next three months, and we will probably be learning from each other too. I will not treat you any differently, you can be sure of that. I am really pleased that I met you. Of course, it's always exciting to meet someone so close to one of your idols, but this will not affect our professional relationship. If you ever feel any differently, I want you to come to me and we can discuss it. Am I understood?" he tilted his head slightly, waiting for me to acknowledge hisstatement.

"Of course. Thank you ever so much. I take my job very seriously, and I appreciate you have the same stance."

After that, Jack and I went through what he expected from me, what tasks he needed me to take care of before he started Monday. He told me tomorrow he would be by for a couple of hours so we could go over his schedule. Then I could fit into his work schedule. We talked for over two hours. When I came out of his office, it was already lunchtime. I rarely took a lunch hour. I would typically go across the road to get a salad or sandwich from the deli, which I loved, and would eat it while working, but today I felt exhausted, probably due to all the emotions I had been through today, so I went and got my sandwich and went for a walk. It was a clear day. It was May, so it was nice to have the sun touch my skin. It wasn't hot, but it was warm enough that I could walk without my coat. When I returned, I sat at my desk and started the desktop up, logged in as usual, and went on with the tasks Jack required. A little later, I went to meet Claire, Mr Reed's PA. She had a pile of paperwork waiting for me. She was lovely, as beautiful as she wassweet.

"I love your shirt, girl. It looks terrific on you. Why have I never seen you before?" Claire asked.

"Thank you. Fashion is something I'm into. You've probably never seen me because I usually come into work and just go across the street to collect lunch and return to work. I never go to the staff room or anything," I told her, feeling a bit shy.

"I understand exactly what you mean. Our job is not very easy, is it? They always need us close by, just in case. Well, it's nice to meet you. We will probably be working together at some point, right? If you're working for Jack and I'm working for his dad, we need to be in sync, girl."

She didn't sound British, but I didn't either, even though I was born in England. I still have a strange accent, which is definitely not Portuguese. It's one of those things I can't understand and can't change.

When I returned to my desk with a file box full of paperwork that I needed to go through before handed it to Jack, I found a vase of huge white roses with a little card. I opened the card.

Dear Isabel,

It will be a pleasure working with you. These are just a small gesture to show my appreciation at your dedication to Reeds Recordings.

Jack Junior Reed

I didn't know what to make of it. The roses were just huge. I mean, I had never seen white roses so big. And there were … sixteen … I counted. I could see he was a kind man; before I even started, he was already showing appreciation. I tried not to think anything of it. It was just a welcome gift, I told myself.

The next day, I parked my car and went outside the Reeds Recordings building, straight to the deli across the road to get my lunch so I didn't have to stop at the lunch hour. I ordered a sand-wich, a juice, and a pack of crisps for myself, and I also ordered two one-crust pie pastries for Jack. He was so nice yesterday, I thought I should return the gesture.

Sitting at my desk, I thought to write him a little note to go with the pastries. I knew he would be coming today for a few hours and thought he might enjoy these fresh pastries. I left them and the note inside his office on his desk.

It wasn't until 11 a.m. that Jack came in. He came in a rush, with just a brief hello, hardly glancing my way, but when he was at his office door, he briskly turned to me and said, "Isabel, if by any chance, main reception calls you saying there is a Mrs Reed to see me, please make sure they don't send her up. If she does come up, please make sure she leaves. Tell her I'm in a meeting or some-thing. Is thatunderstood?"

He was pissed, I could see it. His eyes were almost black, and his voice was clipped. "Of course, Mr Reed," I said, going for pro-fessionalism. He gave me a kind smile.

"Isabel, it's Jack, not Mr Reed. That is my father. It makes me feel old, and I am not old." He had that cheeky smirk back, and I smiled at that.

"Of course, Jack. I'll keep Mrs Reed at bay." He smiled at me again and went into his office without another word.

CHAPTER 6

Jack

Jessica is such a pain in the ass. I cannot believe she's refusing to sign the divorce papers again. She is messing with me, and I know exactly why. She knows I will be taking over my father's business, and she wants shares in it, which I will not allow. I already offered her the amount she wanted a month ago, and now she's coming up with this shit. I am beyond upset. I feel like I want to punch something or someone, but I need to keep it cool. I have too many responsibilities now, and I will not let her deter me. I will not give her shares in Reeds Recordings—that is not negotiable.

I am so out of it that I treated my new PA Isabel rudely. When I sat on my desk, I noticed a brown box and a small card on top, I opened it:

Dear Jack,

Thank you for the lovely roses yesterday. It was very kind of you. I know these are not as pretty, but I hope you enjoy them, as they are my favourites.

Isabel

When I opened the box, there were these delicious-looking pastries. It made my mouth water. I smiled, thinking how sweet she was. She really was something all right. I popped my head out the door and looked at Isabel. She was so engrossed in her work, with her large glasses on her nose, I almost turned away, but I needed to thank her for the pastries.

"Isabel." She looked up, surprise showing on her face. "Thank you for the pastries. They look and smell delicious. I will have them later." She smiled a kind smile.

"Please, you don't have to thank me. The pastries are not like the roses you gave me," she said, pointing at the large vase of white roses she had arranged on the little coffee table between her desk and my office. I also noticed she had rearranged and redecorated the area. There were two comfortable white leather chairs with silver pillows, each chair on opposite sides of the coffee table. On the coffee table was the rose vase and a cardholder with business cards, some magazines, and the newspaper. Behind her, in the corner, was a large silver lamp, and her desk was completely organized with accessories in white and silver tones. It all looked very professional but elegant as well.

"I see you have good taste not only in pastries but also in decor." "You like?" she asked shyly.

"Very much so. Well done. I hope you didn't spend all day yesterday doing this," I said with a littlehumour.

"Oh, no, no, of course not. I did quite a few of the tasks you asked me to. They are nearly complete. In fact, today by 3 p.m., I am sure all will be on your desk for you to go throughtomorrow."

I was impressed at how fast she managed to do what I requested, as well as decorate this working area.

"Well, I will be staying today until about 5 p.m., so I can probably go through it today." I hadn't intended to stay that late, but now I was excited to see what she'd done.

"Also, would you mind if I changed few things on the layout of this floor? I think is not very well designed. As you know, you will have important people coming in to meet you, and the first thing they'll see is a huge station with a loud noise from the workstations. You will have to authorize works, and you will have to spend a small amount of money for works to be done, but I think it will improve the way people view Reeds Recordings when they come in to see you."

Wow, she is smart, and thinking outside her own job description. I like her. That's what I need, someone with great ideas.

"That sounds wonderful, and don't worry about money. Could you get in touch with our interior designers and go over your ideas and costs with them. When you have come up with something that you think is more effective, please run it by me. Once more, thank you for a fantastic job." With that, I turned and went into my office.

At 3.10 p.m., a light knock sounded at my door. "Come in."

"Hi, Jack. It's only me. I have everything you asked for," Isabel said, coming in with a large pile of paperwork, all divided into sections. "Right, so this is the schedule for next week. You have access on your desktop as well, as I just shared the file. If you need me to add anything else to it, please let me know and I'll be happy to do so. Also, these are all our artists' records for the last five years. I know it's a lot, but I also added the ones we are in the process of acquiring, and they are clearly labelled."

Well, she is thorough—I can see that. Another thing I like.

"These are the records for the artists you will be meeting for the next three months, so when you meet them, you know exactly who they are and how well they are doing. Finally, these are the businesses you are acquiring and the ones Mr Reed wants to acquire. I also added the financial situation for each of the business—latest projections and so on. Simon, our financial analyst, got them for me."

Wow, she keeps impressing me. She is very good at her job.

I looked at her, and she looked tired, but she had a huge smile on her face, which made me smile in return.

"Isabel, I can see how hard you worked, and everything seems to be in the order I asked. Leave it with me. It will probably take me a couple of days to go over them. I will most likely be here tomorrow and Saturday all day too, but this is exactly what I need. Thank you."

Friday morning came, and I was early at the office. It was 7.30 a.m. when I came in, and Isabel hasn't arrived yet, as her shift starts at 8 a.m., so I went through the paperwork she handed me the day before. I was amazed at how everything was in detail and at how much research she must have done. I was sure she had worked from home too, because I doubted she could have done all this in one day. At around 8 a.m. a soft knock on my door sounded.

"Come in," I said.

"Good morning, Jack. I thought you might need some fuel for the day. I don't know what you drink, but I just went for the strong black kind. Hope it is to your liking. If not, I have a tall latte as well." She lifted both hands with a cup to go held in each.

"Thank you, Isabel. That's too kind. I'll take the strong black kind," I said while I got up and around my desk.

"Great, there you go." She handed the right one to me, and our fingers brushed against each other. I felt this small twist in my gut, and I felt something else stirring, which embarrassed me, so I turned quickly to my desk and sat again.

"Also, I would like to ask if you have anything that needs my attention. If you don't, I will be meeting with the decorators today. I will make sure by the end of today you have a couple of options for the layout and everything that will involve."

"I am still looking through what you handed in yesterday, so you can get on with the little project. If by any chance I need anything, I'll find you—no worries."

"Oh no, I won't need to leave my station. I will be meeting with them at my workstation so I can monitor who comes in and out. As I assured you yesterday, I will deal with a certain person as per your request," she said with a mischievous smirk. She looked adorable, and I immediately looked at her lips. God, help me, this is so hard, and I don't know why. I will have to call Ian to speak to him. I need someone to talk about what I'm feeling towards Isabel. I need to keep things professional, but I don't know how, because every time I speak to her, I just imagine her lips on mine, my hands on that beautiful body of hers. God ... I am going crazy.

"Hmm, Jack, you okay there? I didn't say anything wrong, did I?"

She looked concerned. Then I realized why. I had my hands balled into fists so tight that my knuckles had turned white. I relaxed them.

"Yes, yes, sorry. I was just thinking about something else."

I needed to tell her who Mrs Reed was. I wasn't sure why, but I needed to let her know.

She was already turning to go.

"Isabel, one more thing. Mrs Reed is my wife … or ex-wife … or soon-to-be ex-wife. We are in the process of divorce. It is a complicated divorce, hence why I don't want to see her here in my workplace." I was so nervous I started to fidget with my hands. Isabel was quiet for a while, just looking at me. I tried not to look into her eyes, as I was afraid of what I would find there.

"Jack, you didn't have to explain it to me. I see that this is affecting you, and as your PA, I will do anything to ease this burden from you. I think keeping your personal life away from your business life is a very commendable thing to do. I can assure you, she will not enter your office without you saying so."

She said this in such a confident voice, I couldn't help but look into her eyes. I saw such confidence in them. She is a strong woman. It made my heart jump.

"Thank you, Isabel. Okay, so I will wait for your input on the project we discussed."

With that, she gave a little nod and went on her way. I just stared at her retreating backside, and I wished I hadn't, because it made me hard as hell. Her ass is so round and perky.

Shit, I need to talk to Ian ASAP.

I dialled his office number.

"Ian Blackwell's office. Mia speaking." Mia was his PA. "Hi, Mia. It's Jack. Is Ian available?"

"Hi, Jack. Let me check. Just a moment, please. Jack, I'll put you through." "Thanks."

"Jack, how are you?" Ian said

"Hi, Ian. I'm good. Well … I don't know, actually. I need to talk to you about something, but I don't want it to be on the phone. Can you meet for drinks at WAX tonight—let's say 7 p.m.?"

"Sure, seven is okay with me. Does it have to do with Jessica? Is she being a bitch?"

"She is being a bitch, yes, but that is not what I need to talk to you about. It's something that is eating at me, and I don't know what to make of it or how to deal with." I sounded defeated.

"Okay, I can sense it's something important. We can talk later. Whatever it is, we can shed some light on the subject. See you later, mate."

"Great, see you."

It was a long day, and I thought Isabel had left for the day, but when I stepped out of the office to go home, I found her at her desk with a few papers scattered atop her desk, typing furiously. I looked at my watch.

"You still here, Isabel? It's six. Didn't you have to leave at five?" I gave her a surprised look

"Oh, Jack, I'm sorry. I didn't see you there. Well, not really. My little girl today is going to stay at my mum's. I just wanted to finish the proposals so you can have a look over the weekend, as you said you would be at the office on Saturday."

"Well, I'm sure that can wait. Go home. I'm sure you have more important things to do." "Actually, I don't. When Lara goes to spend the weekend with my mum, I normally either stay late on Fridays or take work home, so there is not a lot for me to do on those weekends. Don't worry about me. Anyway, I just need five more minutes, and I'll be done for the day." She got back to work.

I wanted to invite her for drinks, but I thought that wouldn't be appropriate, seeing that I'm her boss—even though employees do sometimes go for drinks together on Fridays after work.

"Isabel, I'm meeting a friend at WAX for drinks in a bit. Would you like to tag along? He would be pleased to meet you, I'm sure."

She looked at me with a shocked expression, opening and closing her mouth a few times, trying to decide on an answer.

"Thank you, Jack, but I need to finish this, and then I have a few things to do at home.

Thank you, though." She said this too quickly, looking at the papers instead of me. I felt deflated. I was actually looking to spending time with Isabel outside work, but I think she made the most sensible decision.

CHAPTER 7

Isabel

I didn't know what to say when Jack asked me to after work drinks. In all honesty, I wanted to jump at the chance, but I couldn't do that. He is my boss, and I keep my personal life totally separate from my work. He seemed disappointed, I could tell, but this was for the best.

When I got home, I put my running gear on and went for a run. I was exhausted, but I needed to clear my head, and the best way to do so was to run.

I was listening to "Queen of the Clouds" while running alongside the river Thames. It was a warm evening, with a fresh breeze, which is lovely when you are running. This was good. I was feeling so much more relaxed. Even though all my muscles in my body were screaming at me, I felt refreshed. When I was close to my house, ready to cross the street, a black Jaguar four-by-fourwith tinted windows stopped alongside me.Thedriver window rolled down. It was then that I saw who itwas.

"Jack?"

"Isabel, well this is a pleasant coincidence." Jack was grinning like crazy, and I noticed another gentleman on the passenger seat. He was also very handsome indeed. I would say he was in his early thirties, with light blond spiked hair, blue eyes, and a smile that was worth a million pounds. Yes, he was gorgeous, in a rich kind of way. He was smiling at me, and yeah, he was checking me out, which made me feel very self-conscience.

Jack must have noticed me looking to his friend because he turned and said, "Isabel, this is Ian, my best friend. Ian this is Isabel." He seemed to want to tell him more but left it at that.

"Oh, Isabel, yes, *your PA*. Yes, yes, Jack has mentioned." I was surprised by that and look at Jack. He looked a bit embarrassed.

"So you run? Was this what you blow off us boys for?" He had that cheeky grin again, which made my knees weak.

"Well, kind of. Sorry, but I need to blow off some steam, and the best way for me is not drinking. In fact, I don't drink alcohol at all. My thing is running." I noticed Jack's eyes were racking my body, which left me all shy, so my voice was lower than usual. I usually have an answer for everything, and I am very confident, but Jack makes me feel like a teenager, all shy and insecure—of what, I don't know yet.

"Do you need a ride? Do you live far? I can drop you off," he said, this time looking into my eyes.

"No, no, I live just across the road. No need for a ride, thanks. It was nice to meet you Ian. You boys behave now. Bye." I don't know why I said that last bit. What is wrong withme?

"Oh, we will behave. Don't you worry, Isabel. If not good, we'll be bad," Ian said with a wink.

"See you Monday, Isabel," Jack said, also with a wink. What is it with them and winking?

I am sure it is a thing between them. I gave them a little wave and crossed the road to my place. Only when I was in my drive did they leave. When I got inside, I dropped to the floor with my back to the door. God, he is so ... oh, I don't know what he is. I need to go on a date to take my mind off Jack, and I know the right person to help me with this.

Lizzy answered her phone on the second ring. "Izzy, you okay?"

"Hi, Lizzy, I need your help."

"Oh, that ought to be good. What kind of help?"

"I need you to set me up on a date with that hunk of a guy Mark arranged for me Tuesday who I stood up. I know, I know what you are going to say, but this is me desperate now."

She was quiet for a little while.

"Izzy, what is happening? Something must have happened because you do sound desperate, and that never happens, not about guys." She knew me so well.

"Fine, I think I have a thing for my boss." Another pause.

"You've fallen for Mr Smith?" She sounded shocked, and of course, she would be, as Mr Smith was married, but what she didn't know yet was that I work for Jack now, so I went ahead and explained everything.

"Thank God. You got me worried there for a while, Izzy. Is this boss, Jack, single?"

"Well, yes ... no ... kind of ... He is in the process of divorcing his wife. It doesn't look very good between them, but that is not why I don't want anything to happen between us. The reason is that he is my *boss*, Lizzy. I can't get involved with my boss. I love my job too much to lose it over this."

"Well, the way I see it. You won't be losing anything; you will be gaining. He is your boss.

He's probably a busy person and doesn't have much time for a girlfriend, but if you date him, then you have a way of spending time with him. You both just need to work it out. That's all, babe." Lizzy is such a romantic at heart.

"Lizzy, *no*. I do not mix work with personal—that's also the reason I haven't got them to check Lara's portfolio. I don't want them to do anything for me just because I work for them. I need to find a lovely man to help me separate the two. Will you help or not?" I said this more like a growl.

"Okay, okay, just come down, Izzy. He has got under your skin, hasn't he? Let me see what I can do. But please don't let me down this time."

"I won't. Just get me the date, and I promise I won't let you down. Love you. Mwah."

We ended the call, and I sprinted to the shower. After shaving my legs, underarms, and bits, I plucked my eyebrows and put on a facial mask just as my phone went off.

"Hi, babe," I said to Lizzy.

"Okay, so tomorrow at eight he'll pick you up for dinner and after-drinks. Now, he is a gentleman. He is a professor, just like

Mark. He is thirty-eight, but he looks really good. I have met him, and I can tell you, he is fit."

Okay, so this is it. Tomorrow I will start dating someone other than Jack. Great, fantastic … Shit … shit, I am going on a date …

"Izzy, you not freaking out, are you? Please don't tell me you're freaking out. He is the same guy you were going to meet Tuesday, so it's not like you didn't hear about him before. You okay? If you can't do this, it's okay. I'll just embarrass myself again and cancel."

"No, it's okay. I will be there at eight. Lizzy, I am not going to lie. I am really nervous and scared. It's been … it's been too long, and …"

"I know, honey, I know, but you are a great person—beautiful, hot as hell—you'll be fine. Trust me and enjoy this."

"Okay, could you send me his phone number so I can text him to confirm?" "Yes, sure."

She gave me his number. His name was William. I decided to text him.

> Hi, William. This is Isabel, Mark and Lizzy's friend. I just wanted to confirm our date tomorrow at 8 p.m. I look forward to seeing you then. Thank you. Isabel.

Not long after, I received a text back:

> Hi, Isabel, thank you for confirming, it will be my pleasure to meet you. See you then. Will.

Okay, so he likes to be called Will, not William—noted. Time to go to bed then so I can have a good night's sleep.

When I woke up on Saturday, I was feeling even more tired than when I went to bed. I kept seeing those green eyes of Jack, which were engraved in my soul. Whenever I tried to think of something else, all I saw were those eyes, that cheeky smirk, and that broad shoulders of his. I really didn't know what to do. When I finished cleaning the house, washing, and ironing, it was already 5.30 p.m., so I called Lara, letting her know I would be out and checked to see if she and Mum were okay. My mum was ecstatic to hear I was going on a date. I think she was actually tearing up. Obviously this was a big thing. I haven't seen anyone since Sam, and it's been four years since he died, so yeah, it was a big thing.

At five to eight, as I was just checking my reflection on the mirror, my doorbell sounded.

I rushed to the door.

"Hi, Isabel." In the doorway was this really tall man—tanned, with dark spiked hair and really dark eyes. I would actually say black eyes. He was so broad that he must have been into bodybuilding. He did not look like a professor at all, more like a bouncer—in a sexy way, though.

"Hi, Will. It's nice to meet you," I said with a small voice, feeling a bit intimidated by his size and bulk. I put my hand out, and he took it gently, planting a kiss on top.

"Please, the pleasure is all mine." He looked into my eyes with a smile. He had really nice teeth, too. Oh, man, Lizzy was right—he was fit.

Will drove into the nice area of London, and he took me to Hamilton Hotel.

"I made reservations at their restaurant. They have a great menu. I love it here. I hope it's okay with you," Will said

"Of course it's okay. It's great. I've heard how good their food is, so thank you." I'd also heard how hard it is to book a reservation here. Will must have connections. Again, I found it strange for a professor at university to have such connections.

When we were seated, Will looked at me with a thoughtful expression. I gave him a little smile and asked, "Is everything okay, Will?" He smiled back and looked down at his hands, which were resting on his lap.

"Isabel, Mark told me you've been a widow for four years, but he hasn't said much more. He thinks you should tell me more if you want to. I guess what I'm trying to say is that I understand this is difficult for you. I know you didn't intentionally stand me up on

Tuesday, but can I ask you what made you want to come on this date today?" He tilted his head slightly to the side and was once more looked into my eyes.

"Well, to be honest, I've wanted to do this for a while now, but it's difficult for me to meet new people. I have an 8-year-old daughter to consider in all this. She was only four when her dad died, and she has only me and my mum in her life. My late husband's parents died when he was young, and his sister lives in Australia, so we are all that my little girl has, so it is difficult for me to bring someone into our lives. I decided to come today because I need to start my life again. I have a fantastic job, a wonderful daughter, and the great house, but I don't have someone to share these great things with, apart from my daughter. I think it's time for me to look for that someone."

Will gave me a knowing smile, reached across the table, and squeezed my hand. It was a nice gesture, and I felt comfortable with him, at ease, as if we had known each other for a while.

The conversation flowed nicely. We laughed at stories we told each other. Will kept trying to find out more about Sam, but I tried not to go there. I didn't want this day to have any sadness, so I tried to avoid it.

When dessert came, we shared, just like a couple would. I guess it was a perfect date. He was funny, attentive, sweet, and polite, and we felt really comfortable around each other. When we were leaving, we passed a table with people I recognized at once. Mr Reed, Jack, Ian, Mr Smith, and Mrs Smith. As I caught Jack's expression, I noticed he wasn't happy, but he gave me a small smile."

"Isabel, is that you?" Mr Smith said.

"Hello, Mr Smith, Mrs Smith, Mr Reed, Ian, Jack." I acknowledged everyone with a polite smile and nod.

"You look marvellous, darling. That dress must be Valentino. I know his sexy work," Mrs Smith pointed out.

"Yes, thank you, Mrs Smith. It is Valentino. I do love his work." I briefly glanced in Jack's direction. He was staring at William.

"I'm sorry. How rude of me. This is my date, William. Will, these lovely people are ... well, my boss, Jack, my boss's boss, Mr

Reed, my previous boss, Mr Smith, and his lovely wife, Mrs Smith, and finally, Ian—he is Jack's friend." Everyone laughed when I referred to Mr Reed as "my boss's boss".

"Hello, everyone. It's nice to meet you all." He was so poised and so confident. "Sorry, son, we only got your first name. William ...?" Mr Reed asked. Will flinched at that and looked at me with what it looked like a nervous laugh.

"It's William Hamilton, sir," Will said, looking at Mr Reed and again at me.

Oh, that's how he got these reservations. Now it makes sense.

Shit, I was at *his* hotel—or his family's hotel—one of the best hotels in London, no less. I gave him a small smile, but it didn't reach my eyes. I averted my eyes quickly and looked to Ian instead.

"I see you are having a lovely dinner, so we won't bother you anymore. Please enjoy your evening," I said, trying to get away as soon as possible. Jack didn't say anything at all, which was weird, because he always talks to me. He kept staring Will down with a frown, and when he caught my eye, he smiled, but it looked like a forced smile, not like the smile I'm used to at all. Everyone gave us a farewell, apart from Jack, who merely nodded my way.

"What a first date. Hey, already met your boss and your boss's boss," Will joked. "Yeah, what a first date."

I couldn't get Jack's expression out of my head. He looked upset and sad. I didn't want to think anything of it, but I couldn't help but thinking, was he upset that I was on a date with Will and sad because ... what? Because what? I was quiet for so long that I jumped at Will's voice.

"So, oh sorry. I didn't want to scare you there," he said, laughing. "You okay, Isabel?

You've been so quiet since we left the restaurant." He was speaking with a soothing voice, like you use to a child or a frightened animal.

"I'm okay, Will. I was just ... never mind. This was a wonderful date. You are a gentleman in every sense of the word. Thank you for taking me out."

"Isabel, you don't have to thank me for taking you out. This was my pleasure. You are such a lovely woman. It would be my loss if I didn't take you out." He parked the car in my drive and looked into my eyes again. Taking my hand in his, he kissed the top and closed his eyes.

"This was definitely the best night I've had with someone in a long, long time, Isabel. Would you go out with me again?" He was almost whispering now, and I heard myself almost whispering too.

"I would love to go out with you again, Will. Thank you."

"Okay, then. I'll call you sometime this week." He let go of my hand and gave me a wide grin.

"Yeah, that sounds good. See you then." I opened the door and stepped out of the car. "Bye, Will. Drive safe."

"Will do. Bye."

And with that, he drove away.

That night, before going to bed, I texted Lizzy, letting her know how wonderful of a time I had with Will and that we would be going out again. She replied immediately, saying how excited and happy she was for me. I thought I would sleep well that night, but I was wrong. Jack's face plagued my night. I didn't know what to make of it. I got up around 6.30 a.m. on Sunday. I decided I would go shopping, maybe buy something for my next date.

When all my shopping was done, I called Lizzy, and we met at Remondi restaurant, one my favourite places.

"So, let's hear it. Come on, I need details, babe," Lizzy said, all excited.

"Well, he is such a gentleman—so attentive, funny, gentle," I said, thinking of the previous night but once again remembering Jack's face.

"But ...? There is a 'but' there—I can see it, Izzy."

God, why does she know me so well? In cases like this, I didn't want her to be so close to me.

"There is no 'but'. I am seeing him again. Just waiting for his call." She looked at me expectantly, so I broke. "Fine, there is a 'but'. Jack was at the restaurant. I only noticed him at the end, when we were leaving. He was there with his father, his best friend, and Mr and Mrs Smith. They were all very happy to see me—apart from Jack." I let out a breath. "He seemed quite upset, and he kept looking at Will's if he wanted to punch him or something. I don't know, maybe was my imagination, but every time he looked at me, he would give me a sad smile, not the smile I'm used to seeing on him. For two nights now I've hardly slept. His eyes and his face keep coming to me, and I can't stop thinking of him during the day. There, is that what you wanted to know?" I said, almost shouting.

"Izzy, calm down, babe. It's okay. No, it is definitely not what I wanted to hear, but that's how you feel, so it's the right thing to tell me. I only care about how you feel. I need you to be always honest with me without feeling you're in the wrong, because you're not. You obviously like Jack—more than a simple crush. This is … serious. Don't downplay it. I understand your position, but you can't control who you fall for. Have you considered how Jack feels about you? Because the way you described his reaction tells me he is probably feeling the same thing for you that you feel for him. Yes, I know you are going to give me that shit and tell me you will not date your boss, but Izzy, don't make a decision that may be the wrong one just because he is yourboss."

"I don't know what to do, Lizzy. I liked Will. He is everything I need, but … Jack is like … He's like … pfffffff … Tell me what to do because I don't know."

"Look, just let things develop with both Jack and Will. See who will steal your heart first. If Jack doesn't advance, fine—you have Will, who I'm sure make you happy—but if Jack starts to show interest, let him. Only then will you know what to do."

Again my best friend made me feel better, as she always does. She is right; it's not as if I'm promised to either of them. I will just go with it. Oh, God, I'm not like this. I'm a woman who makes decisions, not one who lives in limbo, but this is the only way.

"Okay, fine. I'll just take it as it comes."

"I know where my money is, but we never know. You might surprise me yet," she said with a smirk.

Later, I went by my mum's to pick up Lara. They were so excited that I enjoyed my date that Mum was already talking about wedding dresses. At that point, I grabbed Lara, and we said our goodbyes.

"Mommy?" Lara pulled my attention to her from driving. "Yes, darling."

"What are you thinking?"

"What do you mean, baby? What am I thinking?"

"There is something bothering you, I can tell. You have that funny face." Lara always says I make a funny face when I am thinking hard.

"Oh, nothing, sweetie. It's nothing. Mummy just has a few things that need to be sorted—that's all." I gave her a reassuring smile, but I could see she didn't buy it. She didn't push it, though. When did she grow up so quickly? She is starting to have conversations like adults and understands so many different emotions. I can't believe she is this big and this intelligent.

CHAPTER 8

Jack

"Jack, you're going to punch a hole in that bag if you carry on like that," Ian said from behind me.

I was so pissed off when I left the Hamilton Hotel, I had to come and work out my frustration. My apartment has its own gym, so that's what I did when I got home, I didn't even close the front door or speak to Ian. I came straight up to work out. I didn't answer Ian; I needed to be in control of my thoughts first.

"Wanna talk about it, mate?" he asked.

"Talk about what, exactly?" I asked while still punching the bag.

"Come on, mate. I know you well. Seeing her with William Hamilton pissed you off so much so that you haven't said a word since dinner."

"Fine, I am pissed off. She is ... well, you've seen her twice now. What do you think?"

I was curious to find out what he actually thought of Isabel. I had told him what I had been feeling and all, but he didn't know her. Only after drinks did he meet her briefly, when I spotted her on the road on her run. She was so sexy in those tight leggings and tanktop. Today too in that sexy-as-hell tight, open-back dress.

"What do you want me to tell you?" "Well, what do you think of her?"

"She is gorgeous. Yes, hot as hell, very elegant—"

"Stop, I know all that. What I'm asking is, what do you think of the way she looks at me?"

"Ah, why didn't you ask that to begin with?" he said with a grin. "There is chemistry between you two, for sure. I could see it both times I met her. She was on a date with William Hamilton, but when she saw you, her eyes had a different light to them. She looked guilty, almost as if she felt she were cheating."

"That's what I felt too, but when we arrived, I saw the way he was making her laugh, and they looked so at ease with each other. They were sharing fucking dessert. I am losing my mind here, Ian. I don't understand why she makes me feel like this. Ever since the first time I literally crashed into her, I can't get her out of my head. She is my PA, so I can't date her—it's not ethical—but I can't not date her, because I can't get her out of my head."

"Okay, so if you know what you need, what are you asking me?" Ian said with an amused smile.

"I guess I need to hear someone who knows me tell me what to do."

"Ah, but I won't tell you what to do because you already know what to do. You like her, and you are going to woo her. That is what you are going to do, isn't it?"

I paused and gave the bag one final punch.

"Fuck, yes, I'm going to woo her. William might have an advantage over me, but I want her, and I will get her."

"There you go. Isn't it so much better talking through things than punching the shit out of this poor bag?" We both laugh out loud at that.

I had to formulate a plan to win her. She seemed to have feelings for me—at least an attraction, but she is holding back, and I am assuming it's because I'm her boss. She is professional, and she doesn't seem the kind of woman to mix personal with professional.

Maybe if I give her more a bigger workload and she has to work longer hours, or even some weekends, we will spend more time together. Maybe that will bring her closer to me.

I emailed her tonight to give her a few tasks before I got in.

Dear Isabel,

I hope you had a lovely weekend. I need you to look into a few things for me, first thing Monday. I will need to meet with you at some point Monday too, so please check your schedule and fit our meeting in. If my schedule is full, please arrange something after working hours. Here are the tasks I need done:

- Call Mrs Corner, my solicitor, and let her know that I need the case pushed forward and that I am happy to go ahead with plan B (she will know exactly what plan B is).

- Confirm reservations for two people the following Saturday evening at the National Music Awards. We are both attending. Hope this is okay with you. I need you there. Will explain later at our meeting.

- Call Carol from Shic and have her arrange both my and your outfit for the awards. She has my measurements and knows what I like. You, on the other hand, will probably have to meet with her.

- I also need to speak with our two last acquired studio's management team, so please arrange a meeting. You will also be present.

- I need to go through the new office layout designs you have left for me. I would like to be a bit more involved with it.

Thank you for your time and attention. I look forward to meeting with you on Monday.

Kindest regards,

Jack

I stepped onto my floor at Reeds Recordings, and when I saw Isabel, I almost had a heart attack. She looked so sexy. Shit, she was doubled over the vase on the small coffee table, wearing a tight red knee-length dress and black high heels. She was a bloody vision. When she turned, she gave me an apprehensive smile. She was wearing red lipstick. Her short light brown hair was straightened, and the left side was tucked behind her ear.

"Good morning, Isabel. How are you in this wonderful sunny day?" I said with a chirpy tone.

She seemed taken aback by my attitude.

"Oh, I'm okay, Jack. How are you?" She had a little frown on her face.

"I'm super now that I've seen you." She widened her eyes, surprised at what I said. I turned toward my office.

"Did you get my email, Isabel?"

"Yes, sir. You have the updated schedule on your desktop. Also already confirmed our presence at the National Music Awards. I will get the other tasks ready …"

I didn't let her finish. Instead, I closed the office door and went to my desktop to see the schedule. I knew I didn't have any slots today, and she would have to either stay after work or we would need to meet in the evening. She has booked our meeting for 7 p.m. There was a note underneath which said,

I will be leaving at 5 p.m. as per usual but will return for the meeting.

Maybe I have been unfair. She has a little girl who needs looking after. Should I just cancel this meeting? I'll speak to her in little bit.

There was something she said before I came into my office that I didn't like. She called me "sir", the same way she did when we first met. It's as if she's trying to distance herself.

At lunchtime, I was about to call Isabel to see if she could get me something to eat, as I was famished. I had been so busy that I didn't even get a minute to have a coffee, but Isabel beat me to the punch. She knocked on my office door.

"Come in."

"Hi, Jack. I took the liberty of ordering some lunch for you. I know you've been extremely busy and will be in meetings all afternoon, so I thought you needed an energy boost." She brought in two bags—one was Indian and the other Chinese.

"I didn't know what you like, so I just bought two different kinds of food," she said with a smile.

"Actually, I like both, but this is far too much food for me to eat alone. Would you eat lunch with me?" *There we go. That wasn't so difficult.*

"Yeah, sure. Thank you," she said a little shyly. She started to lay the food on the large coffee table in my office, and we sat on the leather sofa side by side. Her perfume was sweet and was trying to claim my soul. I felt something in my pants twitching and moved forward with my elbows on my knees so I could hide my excitement.

"Can we share? I love both Indian and Chinese as well."

"Of course. Let me get the drinks. What do you like? I have flavoured water, still water, soft drinks, and whisky—oh, and Champagne too." I wiggled my eyebrows, trying to make her laugh, which she did.

"A soft drink will be fine. I don't drink alcohol, remember?" she said with a quirk of her eyebrow, still smiling.

"Yes, I do remember actually. You should smile more. You look beautiful when you do … I mean, you always look beautiful, but … but when you smile …" I sounded panicked. I felt panicked. What was I saying? God, why do I have to mumble?

"Thank you." Isabel's cheeks were almost the same shade as her dress. I'd made her uncomfortable.

"I'm sorry. I shouldn't have said that. But it's the truth though," I said, looking into her eyes. We were just looking at each other for a little while. I felt the heat coming from her. She was breathing a little faster. I could see her chest rise and fall in rapid succession, and I started to lean in slowly, far too slowly. Isabel broke the silence and brought me out of the daze I was in.

"Which is your favourite Indian dish?" She looked at the food and was dishing out two plates. I cleared my throat.

"I like a few, but if I had to choose, probably lamb balti. And you?" She looked at me, surprise again showing on her face. "What? Is that a bad dish?" I asked.

"No, not at all. It's just, that's my favourite too." We smiled at each other. "What is your favourite Chinese dish then?" I asked her.

"Well, I have to say, I don't have a favourite. I love them all. Why are you looking at me like that?" she said, seeing the "come on" look on my face. "It's true. I don't have a favourite Chinese dish. I love them all."

"Okay, okay, I'll take that. Now I know when I take you out, a safe choice will be Chinese then." I let it slip, wanting to see her reaction.

"Well it seems it is, and may I say, I love Ying Gin—that's my favourite Chinese restaurant. That should make it even easier." I was not expecting *that* reaction.

"Well, thank you for letting me know. Maybe I will be taking you there soon." We both laugh. This was starting to look more like a first date than lunch between a boss and a personal assistant.

"So, Jack, I wanted to run something by you. I have booked our meeting for today 7 p.m., but I can't find anyone to have Lara that late. Will it be okay to bring her with me? She will stay at my desk doing her homework, so she won't bother us. You will not even know she is there." She lookedanxious.

"Of course I don't mind. It will be great to met her. I love children. I always wanted at least a couple. I thought I would be a father sooner, but my ex is not the motherly type. In a way it was a good thing we didn't have any children, because they would be in the middle of a war right now, and that would break me completely." I don't know why I said this to her, but it felt comfortable to confide in Isabel.

"It must be difficult to get divorced. I mean, when I look at my loss ... it wasn't our choice, of course, but divorcing someone you love must be as hard," she said with sympathy in her voice.

"Well, I did love Jessica. I was completely in love with her. She used to be my everything. But I was blind. She cheated on me with Ian's younger brother, Seth. I found them in our family manor together, fucking like rabbits. I just stood there looking on, not believing what I was seeing, you know. She actually laughed and asked if I wanted to join in, as if it were all a big joke to her. That's what broke my heart. If she had apologized or cried and asked for forgiveness or something, I don't know, maybe I would've taken her back. We could have worked it out. But she pissed on my head, made a mockery out of my love for her."

Isabel had her hand on her chest, and I noticed her eyes had unshed tears.

"That is horrible, Jack. I'm so sorry. I cannot imagine what that must have felt like. You are a kind man—anyone can see that—and if she let you go, then she is a fool, a real fool. I would never in a million years would have ..."

She seemed to catch herself, and she looked at her food.

"I'm sorry. I just don't understand how people take marriage so lightly. Marriage is not easy. It has tough moments, but the couple has to work together, even though sometimes one has to give in so the other can be what they are truly born for. I gave up my career for Sam because I loved him. He was a wonderful husband and father—he really was—but I am not stupid or naive. I know he spent a lot of time alone, away from us, and there were maybe a few girls ... Don't look at me like that. He didn't have sex with them, but he did flirt, and maybe more than flirt, but he never had sex with them. I understood the lifestyle his career offered was sometimes enticing, but as a couple, we worked it out. It wasn't easy for me, no, but we just worked through every obstacle, and he always come home back to us. I loved him, and he loved me. For me, that was enough—most of the times." Sadness overcame her as she opened herself to me.

"Isabel, I cannot imagine any man looking at another woman when they have you. You are intelligent, beautiful, loving, kind, and sweet—and you have a rocking body, by the way." I laughed, and she smiled. "Let's just say, if I had been Sam, I wouldn't be looking around, because I would only have eyes for my wife." We were then quiet until we finished our lunch. After we tidied up the leftovers, Isabel was about to leave my office.

"Isabel, thank you for ... the food ... and for opening up to me. I'm really enjoying getting to know you—other than just professionally. You are a wonderful person." Isabel smiled again.

"Thank you Jack. Likewise. Jack ... you will find someone that is worthy of your heart—I am sure of it!" With that, she closed my office door. I did believe what she said, because I felt it already. She was the woman worthy of my heart, and I would give it to her—not just my heart but all of me.

The day went by in a blur. I couldn't take the image of Isabel's lips from my mind. I wanted to kiss her so badly at lunchtime. I could see she wanted it too, but she held back. She is obviously scared, which is understandable. I mean, I am her boss, and she takes her job very seriously, one of the things I love about her. What am I saying? Love? One of the things I *like*, not love.

I had been on a call when there was a soft knock on my door. I looked at my watch. *Oh shoot, it's already 6.55 p.m. That must be Isabel.*

"Hold on, Arnold," I said. Arnold is one of the new studio's managers we recently acquired in Florida. "Come in." Once Isabel came in, I gestured for her to wait a minute and pointed to the sofa for her to take a sit. "Yes, Arnold. I think I can fly over sometime this month. I'll get my PA to organize it. She will get in touch with you with all information you requested.

And Arnold, I want you to go ahead and sign the little boy. All right, look, I have an important meeting. Isabel will be in touch soon. See you, mate. You too." I ended the call and gave Isabel a grin.

"So, Ms Winter, how are you this evening?"

"Hi, Jack. I'm great, thanks. Should we start then?" She was looking into a file she brought in.

"Wait a second. Didn't you bring someone to work with you, someone who is kind of small and related to you?" I said, trying to get her to look at me, which she did.

"Lara is just outside the office, at my desk. Oh, you wanted to meet her. Right, okay, then." She was nervous, I could tell. She got up, and I followed her.

"Lara, sweet pea, this is Jack, my boss. Jack this is Lara, my sweet pea," she said, smiling broadly

"Hello, Mr Jack. Nice to meet you, sir." She was so cute and so polite. Her mother really is wonderful at everything.

"Hello, Lara. Please don't call me 'sir'. I am not that old," I said, making a face. She laughed at that.

"Well, my mummy always says that I need to treat gentlemen by 'sir' and ladies by 'madam', so I have to call you 'sir'. Tell him, Mummy." She looked at Isabel.

"Yes, that's right, sweet pea, but if jack is asking you not to call him sir, it's okay. Just call him Jack." She looked at me with a kind smile.

"Great, that means I'll be your friend, Jack," she said with a smile. She gave me a little hug as Isabel blushed.

"Of course. We are now pronounced friends," I said, which earned me two lovely laughs from mother and daughter alike. How happy I felt at this moment. My heart felt full. I can't explain this feeling. It just seemed content. All was in place.

"Okay, Lara, I will be just inside going over a few things. It should be about forty-five minutes, okay, darling?" Isabel said to Lara. She nodded.

We were inside my office when I said, "She is lovely, Isabel. She has your eyes." "Well, that is about it, I think. She is like her father—an easygoing, happy little thing."

She looked happy, but she also had a trace of sadness to her smile. "So, this project. Here are a few ideas we came up with. As you can see, there is the quote at the end in detail. I tried to get the best out of the layout without disrupting the workdays. The contractors and designers are very happy to do all work over next weekend so that on Monday, when everyone is back, it will be a normal working day, just at different workstations. I can email everyone on this floor letting them know that there will be some work done and that their workstations will be stated on a board at the floor entrance. That will help everyone not to get confused. What do you think?" She looked up with uncertainty from the sheets laid on the table.

"Wow, Isabel, these are amazing. Are these all your ideas?"

She nodded and then went on, "Well, most of them. The designers helped with colours, patterns, and little bits and bobs. I personally prefer layout two. It's more like a long-term thing. I don't think you'll need to change it around for a long time, to be honest. And also, if you see what I've done here, I created my workstation to be bigger, so if we need to have someone else in the future work alongside me, there is the space for it. What do you think?"

"I agree with you. Let's go for layout two, but can we add a few small coffee stations around the floor. It will help people since they won't have to go around to the end to get a coffee if they need one."

"Yes, of course. I'll let the designers know and book them for next weekend. Anything else you'd like to discuss?"

"Yes, I just wanted to know how you find it working for me."

I needed to know if I was overloading her with tasks beyond her responsibility.

"I am enjoying it very much, actually. It's kind of exciting to start projects, and I have learned a bit more about other areas, which is great for my future, of course." She was happy— I could see it in her eyes.

"Great. Isabel, I need to talk to you about something that's been on my mind since I first met you." I was sweating, so I wiped my forehead with my thumb. "I know I'm your boss and all, but I need to be honest and tell you ... I fancy you." I looked her in the eye. I wanted her to know every word I was saying was true. "I can keep our personal relationship and our work relationship separate. I know what you are thinking, but it won't affect your work at any point, trust me. I would like to go out with you on a few dates outside work, if you'll let me." She was staring at me with her lips slightly parted. Then she gave me a small smile.

"Okay."

Wait, what?

"Okay? You mean, okay, you will let me take you out?"

I can only hope, right?

"Yes, I think we can go out and see if anything will come out of it. But let's go out as friends and see if it leads to anything more," she said.

"I'll take that. So, can I take you out this Saturday? I'll pick you up, let's say, 7 p.m.?" "Actually, Saturday I have a dinner booked with a friend. Actually, it's William. You met him before," she said a bit nervously but with a cheeky grin. Was she trying to make me jealous? If so, she had succeeded. I needed to find out more about their relationship.

"Yes, I remember William well. Have you known him long?"

"Not really. I stood him up once. Yeah, I know. My best friend, Lizzy, and her husband, Mark, set us up. William is a professor in the same university where Mark teaches. They figured we were both singles and decided to set us up. The first time I forgot about the date because Lara had rehearsals and extra music lessons. But then I just thought to give it a shot and went out with him. You know, it was the first time I had a date since my husband."

I was pissed. I should have had that first date.

"Well, you are a great woman, Isabel, and I am sure there are lots of men falling at your feet." She was staring at my hands, and I realized I had them balled into fists. I relaxed them and smiled at her.

"Jack ... I like you. You aren't like many men I know. Most are like predators: they see a widow and just think of one thing, sex. I can see you are not like that; otherwise, you would have come on to me quite harshly. You are a gentlemen—I can see that."

Okay, so she thinks I'm a good boy. How wrong she is.

If she only knew what I wanted to do to her right now, she would be running so fast. I gave a little laugh and looked at her eyes, her lips, her hair. She is so beautiful.

"What? Why are you looking at me like that?" she said with a little smile.

"I just think you are so beautiful, and for the life of me, I can't understand how you been alone this long," I said honestly.

"Well, I just wasn't ready, and I never seem to find a nice guy who is actually interested in getting to know me, I guess." She appeared shy as she told me this. "To be honest, it was me. I just wasn't ready, so I never looked around much, and if someone tried to get close, I wouldn't give them a chance. I would just shut it right down. I have Lara to think about, and I just focused on her and my career." She was being so honest that this felt so comfortable.

"I guess you did have a lot going on. Tell you what—I'll leave it in your hands. When you want to have a good night out, call me."

"Perfect. I will most definitely call you. It's getting late for Lara. If we done here, I shall see you tomorrow."

I nodded. Isabel got up, and I followed her out.

CHAPTER 9

Isabel

I was feeling so happy and smiling so much that my face was starting to hurt.

"Sweetie, we are all done now. We can go home," I said to Lara. She was listening music on her iPod.

"Oh, great. I finished my homework, Mummy." She was so good. Thank the heavens for giving me such a responsible little thing.

"Good girl." I turned to Jack, who followed me out. "Jack, I almost forgot, is it possible to leave early this Friday? Lara has a huge performance at the Great Hall. It's being organized by her music teacher, and there will be very important people there. It's kind of a big deal."

Jack gave me a surprised looked. "Does Lara sing?" he asked.

"Well, she has a lovely voice, but she is actually a pianist." I looked at Lara, who looked at Jack all smiles, beaming with pride.

"Wow, we have a performer here then," he said, throwing me what seemed like a frustrated look. I didn't understand why.

"Jack, I'm sorry. I can make my hours up on Saturday. I don't want you to think I am shirking."

He frowned. "Isabel, don't be silly. You already do too much. I am sure you will make up the time. You don't have to worry about that. I just ... can we talk tomorrow? It's late, and it's nothing we can't discuss tomorrow," he said.

"Of course we can. I'll see you tomorrow, Jack." He said good-bye to Lara, and we went home. On the way, Lara was telling me how cool my boss was—and how gorgeous he was—and I just kept quiet because I couldn't argue with that. He is cool and gorgeous. God, too gorgeous. I could lose myself on those eyes of his alone.

On the next day, I arrived at work and started with my daily routine. I had so many emails to sort through, it was like a marathon to get them all sorted. When Jack arrived, he tapped my desk and said for me to follow him into his office. I guessed we were going to finish our talk from last night.

"Have a sit, Isabel." He pointed to the chair opposite his desk, so I took a seat while he went around his desk and sat himself.

"So, how are you today?" He looked really serious, and that made me nervous. Was I in trouble? Shit, is it because I asked to go early Friday?

"I'm okay, Jack, and you?" He looked at his hands and then lifted his head.

"Well, I am kind of upset actually. Yesterday, when I went home, I kept thinking about what you said about Lara performing at the Great Hall, that there would be important people there, and that got me thinking. If she is a performer—and I bet she is good because she wouldn't be able to get a performance at the Great Hall if she wasn't—how come we, as in Reeds Recordings, have never heard of Lara Winter?"

Ah, now I understood why he was upset.

"Jack, I'm sorry if you are upset. That is not what I intended. You see, I don't want Lara to get things easily just because she has a mum who works for one of the biggest recording companies in the world. I want her to work hard and be recognized for her true talent, without giving her everything." I looked at Jack, and he was frowning.

"What? So you are telling me that you have a really talented daughter and you have the means to get her career started in the *best* recording company in the world, and just because you think she should work hard, you won't give her, or Reeds Recordings, that opportunity?

Okay, look, I see that you want to teach your child hard work, and I don't have children, so I can't even say if that is the right thing to do, but as the soon-to-be CEO of Reeds Recordings, I expect anyone who has knowledge of real talent to inform me of such. As Lara is your daughter, I expect you to come to me and at least invite me to a performance so I can actually have the opportunity to see if there is talent there—and if we could potentially sign her up."

He was giving me a serious look.

"I'm sorry, Jack. I never looked at it that way. I guess you're right. I should have at least informed you she had talent and let you make the next move. If it's not too late, would you like come to her performance this Friday at the Great Hall with me? I have four tickets. My friend Lizzy and her husband are attending, so I could use one of the tickets for you."

Jack smiled, and I saw a sparkle in his gorgeous green eyes.

"Perfect. So you will have to go home first to change I'm assuming," he said, all smiles. "Yes, the performance is at 6.30, so I will have to leave around 4 p.m. as I need to pick Lara up and get ready. Should we meet outside the Great Hall? Then we can all go in together. But I have to warn you, I need to be there by 6 p.m. so Lara can prepare."

"I will be there. Now that was a great start to the day," he said, and we both smiled. Later that day, at 5 p.m., I was about to leave when Jack called my line.

"Yes, Jack, do you need anything?"

"I just wanted to check if you sorted the outfits for the National Music Awards yet." "Yes, it's all sorted. They will deliver them early tomorrow—yours at your house, mine at my house. Anything else?"

"No, that is all. You're leaving now, right?" "Yes, I am about to leave."

"Okay then, I'll see you tomorrow, Isabel—and thank you." "See you tomorrow, Jack."

He sounded tired and sad. I wondered whether I should see if he needed to talk but decided against it, just in case he took it in the wrong way, so I left.

Friday was here, and Will texted me early in the morning to make sure I didn't forget our date tomorrow. I wanted to go because he had been such good company the other night, but at the same time, I felt it was wrong because I had feelings for Jack. What those feelings were, I didn't know yet, but there was definitely an attraction there. I ended up confirming the date with Will. I had to see if William made me feel more than what I felt for Jack. William was so gentle and attentive, and he made me laugh—a lot actually. In all honesty, it was more like we were great friends, but it could develop into something more, right? Even when I tried to tell myself that he was just right for me, the only thing on my mind where those green eyes that took my breath away every time I looked at them.

I need to go on a date with Jack too, to at least get clear on my feelings for him. Yes, I'm sure if I go out with him, it will all be clear.

Work on Friday went by fast—I mean, really fast. I hardly realized it was time for me to leave when Jack popped out of his office asking me if I wasn't supposed to be leaving.

"Oh, gosh, I'm running late," I said, looking at my wristwatch. I needed to pick Lara up from school, and we had to get ready. I logged off my computer and put on my cardigan.

"I'll see you in a bit, then," I said to Jack while dashing away from my desk.

"See you in a bit, Isabel," Jack said with that cheeky smirk that made my knees weak. Thankfully I was on time to get Lara from school, which was a miracle considering London's traffic is always a pain in the ass. When we got home, we went straight to get ready, I had Lara's dress ready, hanging in her closet; her shoes were on the floor in her bedroom. She went to shower and I did her hair and applied very light makeup, just a touch of mascara and rosy lip gloss. She looked so beautiful that I almost (almost) cried. Then I went to get ready. I had one of my favourite black dresses ready, a Stella McCartney design. It was long but really fitted, lifting my breasts and hugging my middle section quite well. It emphasized my curves, which were very few really, but this dress actually made it look like I had some. The back had black lace covering my skin and a long golden back necklace. I added long gold earrings and my gold peep-toe high heels. I looked at the mirror as I did my hair and my makeup, which was also very light—only eyeliner, really black to make my eyes stand out. I was happy with the look. I thought of Jack. What would he think of the way I looked? I chastised myself for the thought.

Lara's mouth hung open when I came into the living room. "Mummy, you look so beautiful."

"Oh, thank you, darling. I wanted to make sure I wouldn't embarrass you, so I made a little extra effort. So you think this will do?" I asked, giving a little twirl.

"Mummy, you are going to be the most beautiful person there. Now I don't feel so pretty anymore," she said, looking at herself.

"What? You are like an angel in that sparkling gold dress, sweet pea. You are so beautiful that I almost cried when I saw you." She laughed and came in for a hug. "Are you nervous, sweet pea?" I asked, because for the first time she was fiddling with her hands.

"Well, now that I know, sir ... Jack ... is coming, I am a bit," she said a little too quietly. "Sweet pea, you don't have to be. He is just going to be there as a friend. He liked you, so he wanted to see you perform."

"Yes, I know but he likes you too." She said this so fast that I had to think of what she meant.

"Lara, what are you saying, baby?" I asked, bending to her level.

"Well, I could see it the other day, Mummy. He was looking at you like you were a princess, you know?"

I laughed at that. "Oh, sweet pea, Jack is a kind man—that's all. Now, let's get going or we'll be late."

When we arrived, it was hard to find a parking spot, but in the end, we found one closer to the Great Hall than I expected. I was straightening Lara's dress when she let out a squeak.

"Jack!" She ran into Jack's arms to hug him.

"Hi, Lara. How are you?" he said, giving her a little twirl in the air. She laughed. "I'm excited. I will dedicate my last performance to you, Jack."

"Oh, you're performing more than once?" he asked her.

"Yes, first a well-known piece with a quartet, and before it ends, one original song I wrote. I will be singing while playing too," she said, smiling, showing all her teeth.

"Wow, I can't wait for that." Jack looked surprised. He turned to me. "Hi, Isabel," he said, running his gorgeous green eyes over my body.

"Hi, Jack," I said timidly, fiddling with the front of my dress, smoothing the crease from the drive.

"You look ... phenomenal, Isabel," he said a little too breathlessly.

"Thank you, Jack. You look great yourself in your black tie," I said. He always looks great in his suit, but this was something else. He looked like a sophisticated secret agent—very yummy.

"So should we go? Lara must be inside in the next three minutes, or else she won't have enough time to get ready," I said in a rush. All three of us met Lizzy and Mark outside and went in together. As I dropped Lara backstage, everyone took their seats.

"Sweet pea, break a leg," I told her, as I always did, and gave her a kiss and hug. "Thanks, Mummy. I love you."

"I love you too, sweetheart." I went to take my seat and noticed Lizzy was chatting animatedly with Jack while Mark was looking on with a serious look. My seat was next to Jack, away from Lizzy, who gave me the thumbs up from behind Jack. I felt my face get hot. Jack smiled at me, noticing the colour in my face.

"You okay, Isabel?"

"Yeah, just a bit hot, probably nerves, you know," I said, trying not to look him in the eye. Jack said nothing to that.

"So, you also forgot to mention that Lara writes her own music."

"Well, she actually just started to do that a few months ago. She is good, though. I didn't know she would be performing one of her own today actually."

"Oh, so she didn't tell you?" he said with a little frown.

"No, I found out the same time you did," I said with a little laugh.

"Wow, I do feel special today," he said, looking me straight into my eyes. We looked at each other until the lights went dim and a presenter came out to present the first performance.

Lara gave the best performance of her life. I, as usual, was crying like a baby while Jack held my hand. He was mesmerized by Lara. When she gave her last performance, we were all blown away. Her voice was like an angel. The song she wrote was called "Best Friend in You". I had heard her sing that song a few times before, but only now, as I was actually listening with my whole heart, did I realize it was dedicated to Jack. Lara thought of him as her best friend. My heart couldn't take anymore. He had not only crawled into my heart, but he had done the same to my baby girl. She hardly knew him, and she already saw him as her friend. I looked at Jack, and I almost lost myself at what I saw: he had a tear rolling down his face. He tried to hide it, brushing a large thumb over his cheek, but it was too late. I had seen it. My heart did a dou-ble-flip, something I'd thought it would never do again, the same flip it did many years ago, with my late husband, Sam. The feelings growing inside me were not just attraction; it was becoming more, but it was wrong—surely it was wrong.

I still love Sam. I still think of him as my husband, but looking at Jack now is like ... He makes me feel things I thought I would never feel again, and it scares the shit out of me.

When Lara finished, everyone got up. The clapping and whis-tling and cheering were so loud, and I was so proud of her that I couldn't help crying again. Jack held my hand again, and I felt a tingling sensation creeping up my arm. My whole body seemed to relax at his touch. I smiled at him while wiping my tears with a tissue.

"Isabel, we need to arrange a meeting as soon as possible. I need to sign Lara. She is phenomenal—so talented, and her voice! Her lyrics are genius, absolutely genius."

"Oh, gosh, really? You really like it? I know she is amazing, but I need you to be honest," I said, looking into his eyes to make sure he wasn't lying.

"Isabel, are you crazy? Did we just see the same performance? Lara was amazing. She is so bloody talented that I actually need her to work with us."

I was so happy that I just hugged him tightly. I hadn't even thought about it. When I realized what I was doing, I stepped back and looked to the floor. "I'm sorry, Jack. I shouldn't have. I was just so elated that I ..." I didn't know what to say. I was so embarrassed.

"Hey, Isabel, it's okay, it's fine," he said, lifting my chin with a finger and looking into my eyes. I lost myself again in those gorgeous green eyes.

"Ahem ..."

Someone was trying to get our attention. Of course, it was Lizzy.

"I'm not interrupting anything, am I?" she said, looking at both Jack and me with an amused smirk. This made me blush again.

"No, no, no. Jack was just telling me that he wants to sign Lara as soon as possible, and I just ..." I didn't know what to say.

"I don't want sign Lara; I *need* to sign Lara. Did you see her performances? Wow!" Jack said with a huge smile that lit up his whole face.

"Yes, she is something, all right," said Lizzy.

"We are so very proud of her," said Mark, a bit more relaxednow.

"I still can't believe my little girl is actually going to become famous. I always knew she would make it one day, but it's all so real now," I said and let out a long breath. The next thing I knew, I was being tapped on my shoulder by Lara's teacher, MrsMcCann.

"Isabel, can I steal you for a moment backstage. There are a few people who would like to speak to you."

"Oh, okay." I turned to my guests. "I will be quick. Will you guys wait for me and Lara outside by the entrance while I deal with this?"

They all agreed, and I went backstage, where at least six people wanted to talk to me.

They were recording companies. One was actually Reeds Recordings' competitor. They all wanted to sign up Lara, and they left their cards with me, asking me to please give them a call and arrange a meeting to discuss Lara's brilliant future. I politely thanked them for their interest and let them know I would give them a call. I was so very happy for her. She came skipping to my side.

"Hi, Mummy. What did you think? Did I make you proud?" she said with a toothy smile. "Oh, sweet pea, I am the proudest Mummy in the world. You were so amazing that I couldn't stop crying."

"Well, that is nothing new. You always cry when I perform," she said, hugging me tight. "I do, don't I? Silly me." We both laughed and went out to meet our guests. Jack was chatting happily with Lizzy, and Mark was actually smiling. There was something about Jack that everyone seemed to like. Yes, he was gorgeous and kind, but there was something else that made people like him.

"Hi, guys. So, should we go to dinner?" They all agreed, and we went to my favourite Chinese place. We had such a great night together, laughing. Lizzy kept throwing glances at me with a knowing smile. Mark and Jack were talking about some study that I didn't understand anything about, and I was actually quite impressed with Jack. He knew so much, it was as if he actually studied that stuff. Even Mark seemed impressed with him.

"We have to get together sometime, man," said Mark to Jack.

"Sure, anytime. Give me a buzz. Here is my card. Any time you want go for drinks or something, give me a call," Jack said.

"Oh, you guys are already exchanging numbers—how sweet. Mark doesn't kiss on first dates though," Lizzy said playfully, and we all broke out laughing.

"Mummy, can we all go home. We can watch a movie and eat popcorn," Lara said with enthusiasm.

"Yeah, why not? Guys, will you come and watch a movie with us?" I asked, hoping to God Jack would say yes.

"Yeah, we're down with it," said Lizzy, looking at Mark, who was nodding. I looked at Jack, waiting for his reply.

"Are you sure it's okay? I don't want to be a nuisance or any-thing," he said looking at me.

"Nonsense. We have a home theatre with a popcorn machine and we hardly use it. It'll be fun, right sweet pea?" I said. I was so excited that Jack actually was going to come to our house. But God, was I nervous as hell!

CHAPTER 10

Jack

I was speechless when Isabel invited me into her home for a movie. I guess I couldn't count that as a date because we were with her friends and her daughter, but it was still so exciting to get to know her better. This was the Isabel I wanted to get to know—her personal life including her friends, her daughter. She was actually inviting me into her house.Wow!

When we got there, she had the front door open, and we all stepped inside. From the outside, the house didn't look huge, but when I stepped in, it was a totally different story. The building was traditional Victorian, with huge white pillars at the entrance. The large entrance hallflowed into an open-plan living/dining space. I meanit washuge, like a reception hall, perfect for big dinner parties, all decorated in whites, blacks, andsilvers.

"Wow, Isabel you have such a beautiful house."

"Thanks, I do love it. Let's go down," she said. I follow them to the basement, where there was a long corridor with doors to the left and right. Isabel opened one on the left, which said "Cinema". The cinema room was impressive, with large red leather recliners and a large screen taking up an entire wall.

"Make yourselves at home while Lara and I change into something more comfortable.

Lizzy, the tablet is inside that cabinet. Please choose something we can all watch. I will be down very shortly," Isabel said. Before she left, she gave me a warm smile. "The bar is next door.

Please help yourself to anything you like. If you prefer soft drinks or water, you can find them in the same cabinet where Lizzy got the tablet. She will show you if you need help."

"Thanks, Isabel. Don't worry about me. I'll be fine," I said with a smile while watching her leave.

"So, Jack, how is it to be Isabel's boss?" asked Lizzy with a smirk on her face. I considered the answer for a moment. Truthfully, it was great and horrible at the same time— great because Isabel is amazing at her job and so professional, the perfect PA; on the other hand, it was horrible because every time I was at work I wanted to do things to Isabel that no boss should even think about, like kissing every inch of her body, touching her beautiful tanned skin playing with her irresistible lips and hearing her moan. God, just thinking about it was making me so hard.

Shit, Jack, just answer already— and cross your fucking legs before they notice.

"Isabel is the perfect PA. She is very professional. What more can a boss want?" I said, crossing my legs and smiling at her. Lizzy turned away from me, and I think she said quietly, "I'm sure she is."

We were getting the popcorn out of the popcorn machine when Isabel and Lara came into the room. Isabel was in black leggings and a long loose wool top which reached just over her bottom. She was still wearing makeup, and she looked just as hot as she had earlier. Lara was in her pyjamas, which had music notes all over them. She looked so cute.

"Sorry, guys. I just had to get into something more comfortable," Isabel said, looking at me.

"No worries. Sweet or salty?" I asked both girls. "I want sweet, please," said Lara.

"Me too," said Isabel. I handed over their little parcels of popcorn. Lara sat on my right, while Isabel sat on my left between Lizzy and me. "So, what we watching then?" I asked Lizzy.

"I picked *Coco*, the animated movie. What do you think, Lara?" She squealed with excitement. "Yes, oh yes, please."

We all laughed, and Lizzy started the movie. Throughout the movie, I spent more time watching Isabel than I did the movie. She occasionally glanced my way, and every time our eyes met, we would smile. I so wanted to kiss her lips. My heart was beating so fast, my blood rushing in my veins. I had to restrain myself, but it was becoming almost impossible. I kept thinking of the people who were in the room, and that was the only thing that kept from kissing her.

After the movie, Lara fell asleep. Isabel asked Mark if he could take her up to her room, and Lizzy offered to help, leaving Isabel and me alone.

"So, this is how you live. Very posh you are," I said with an amused tone, turning my body towards Isabel.

"Yeah, yeah, don't get too excited though. I haven't been in this room for … well, almost a year now. The last time was with Lara and Lizzy. Yes, I have a nice house and a comfortable life, but I am not a snob, I can assure you," she said.

I laughed a little at that. "No, you are not a snob." I paused, looking into her eyes. Those golden eyes stared back at me with a look that made my insides jump.

"You are so gorgeous. Did you know that?" I whispered, leaning in a little. "So I have been told," she said a little breathlessly, leaning in just a little too. "Isabel, I so want to kiss you right now—"

I couldn't finish the sentence because Lizzy and Mark walked in at that very moment, breaking the spell we were under.

"Well, we are off. Oh, sorry, did we interrupt something?" Lizzy said cheekily.

"*No*, no, not at all. We were just … talking," Isabel said, turning to her friends quickly.

She was blushing brightly.

"Okay then, so, as I was saying, we are off. We'll leave you grownups to your *talking*." Lizzy grinned at Isabel, which made me laugh. She was such a tease. I liked both Lizzy and Mark. They seemed to be such great friends to Isabel. I didn't want to embarrass Isabel further, so I decided I should go as well.

"I'll go with you guys," I said, looking at Isabel. Her smile seemed to falter for a second, but it quickly returned.

"Oh, okay. I'll show you all out then," she said politely. At the door, I let Lizzy and Mark go a little farther ahead while I stayed behind, leaning against the doorframe. I looked at Isabel.

"Isabel, I want to thank you for the wonderful evening and for the opportunity to attend your daughter's spectacular performance. I do want to work with her, and I want to oversee the process to make sure she becomes the world-famous artist she was born to be," I said, looking straight into her eyes.

"Thank you, Jack. And the pleasure of having you with us this evening was mine," she said, a little quietly, looking into my eyes. Out of the blue, she stood on her tiptoes and kissed my cheek. If only I turned slightly I could capture those lush pink lips of hers, but I had to remind myself there were still people looking on. I needed to show her respect, even if it was killing me not to kiss her then and there, so I just gave her a little smile and whispered in her ear.

"Next time it will be me kissing you, and it will not be on the cheek."

With that, I turned and got into my car, giving her a little wave as I looked into my rear- view mirror. Her expression was shocked, with her hand up to her mouth. I actually had to slam on the accelerator before I changed my mind and went back.

I got home and threw myself onto the bed, closing my eyes, remembering the feel of Isabel's lips on my cheek. She actually gave me a taste, albeit a small one. Those lips were so soft against my skin, I was like a dying man. The only thing that could save me was her. I was so hard thinking of Isabel that I had to alleviate this sexual tension, so I walked into my en suite bathroom, stripped, and turn on the shower. It didn't take long. Just the thought of Isabel's lips kissing and her tongue tasting me did the trick. But even then, it did little to deflate me completely. I still needed her, and I went to bed with a semi hard-on. It was torture falling asleep, and I couldn't imagine how it would be in the morning. Shit, this thing has a mind of its own.

Saturday came and went in a blur. I had drinks with Ian late in the evening. My mood was really bad knowing Isabel was on a date with William Hamilton.

"What's wrong, Casanova? You look like you want to break something," Ian said while taking a sip of his lager.

"Fuck, Ian, I don't know where to start. I am going crazy with thoughts of Isabel. She makes me want her so fucking bad that it physically hurts, man. Yesterday, after her daughter's per-formance—you know, at the Great Hall. I told you this yesterday morning, right? So, after the performance, we went out for dinner with her friends and her daughter. Let me tell you, that little girl is such a joy. She even made me cry at the performance. Yeah, I know. Anyway, after dinner, we went back to Isabel's house—no, scratch that. We went to Isabel's *mansion* to watch a movie in her home cinema. As I was leaving, she kissed my cheek. Pfffff ... I almost lost it, man. I almost turned my head, but then I remembered the friends who were standing in the drive, and I just didn't kiss her. But today she is on a date with William Hamilton, and I feel I was so fucking stupid for not kissing her. She probably wouldn't have gone on this stupid date if I had just kissed her, don't you think?"

I said all this in such a rush that Ian, holding his pint in his hand, just stared at me with his mouth open.

"*Wow*," Ian said, downing half the pint before continuing. "So let me get this right: You are in a shit mood because she is on a second date with William Hamilton, and you think it is your fault because you failed to kiss her."

I simply nodded.

"Jack, look, this is good. She invited you to a dinner with her friends after the performance, which she didn't have to do, and then she invited you to watch a movie at *her house*, and then to top it off, she kissed you. Well, yeah, on the cheek, but I can say you are well ahead of Mr William Hamilton. Don't look at me like that. You are. You met her daughter, for crying out loud, and her close friends—what does that tell you, mate?"

When he put it like that, it did sound as though she was into me and it was progressing quite nicely. But then again, it wasn't a date.

"I have yet to go on a date with Isabel. Please don't forget she is on a date right now with William. What am I suppose to do about that?" I looked at my whisky on the rocks and closed my eyes, thinking of her beautiful golden eyes.

"Well, you have her number, don't you? Even if she's with him, you can make sure her mind is on you, man. Make her want to leave early and speak to you. Like that time with what's her name?

Sunita. Yes, that's right, Sunita at Uni. You spent all night texting her until she asked you over at around two in the morning. Ah, now you remember, right?"

I laughed, remembering our Uni days. They were fun, and life seemed so easy then. No fucking pain-in-the-ass exes or business responsibilities. But Ian was right: I needed to make Isabel want me as badly as I want her. I took a large swig of my drink, got up, and patted Ian's back.

"Thanks, man. I got to go. Call tomorrow, yeah?" I said in a rush, leaving the bar to put my plan into action.

As I was sitting on my sofa watching the TV, I took my phone out of my pocket and started texting Isabel.

Hi Isabel how are u?

Not long after, I got a reply.

I'm okay, u?

My heart was beating so fast as I typed again.

Well I'm better now but could
be even better if I heard your
voice 😊

I waited and waited. I was sure she wouldn't reply, but then a message came through.

Lol you are funny today, are
you drunk Mr Junior Reed?

All right, she was talking.

I did have a couple but no,
no drunk just being honest.

OH I forgot you suppose to be
on a date right?

Again, it took a little while before she replied.

> I am on a date with William,
> now stop distracting me
> cause he actually asked if my
> boyfriend was back from a
> night out and is checking on
> me … lol … I told him it was
> my very demanding boss.

I laughed. I was getting the response I expected. William knew we were texting. Even if he thought it was about work, that made me feel great.

> Well you could just tell him
> to cut the evening short and
> come hang out with me;)

My leg was jerking on its own. I waited for her reply, which seemed to take forever.

> I don't hang out with any-
> one. If you want my company
> you will have to take me on a
> date, sir.

Shit, she did want to go on a date, and here I was, thinking she had blown me off to spend the evening with William. If I'd known, I would have made her cancel her date with William and go out with me instead, but I wanted to give her options, I guess.

> Okay then so tomorrow is
> Sunday lets have lunch I'll
> pick you up around 12 how
> does that sound?

The reply this time was almost instantaneous.

> Great you have yourself a date. Oh by the way just so you know I don't kiss on the first two dates;)

What did she mean by that? She doesn't want me to kiss her or she won't be kissing William tonight?

> Well I will sleep a little better tonight then, as you won't be kissing that loser tonight. But so we are clear I will be kissing you on our first date. Have a good night Isabel.

There were no more replies, but I achieved what I really wanted. She agreed to an official date tomorrow. And to make things clear, I will be kissing her, and she will love it. She will be begging for more, and if she's good, I'll give her more—so much more.

I woke up really early today. I was so looking forward to seeing Isabel, all kind of crazy thoughts were going through my mind when my phone went off. I picked it up on the fourth ring not recognizing the number.

"Hello."

"Hello, baby." The voice that came through was of the last person I wanted to hear this morning—or ever.

"Jessica, what do you want?" I said, well annoyed.

"I was in bed and just thought of you, baby. Jack, why are we getting divorced? Let's work things out. I miss you baby."

I was completely and utterly speechless. What was she on? She had to be on drugs.

There is no other explanation. Mistaking my quietness, she went on.

"Jack, I love you. I know I did a horrible thing, but I want to try and make this marriage work."

"Are you on drugs?" There was nothing else I could say. The way she was going on, that was the only thing that even made sense.

"What? *No*. How can you ask me that? You know I would never do any drugs. They are so bad for your skin."

Okay, now she sounded more like herself.

"Look, Jessica, I expect you to sign the fucking papers Monday. I am so fucking tired of your games. There is no marriage to save. I am truly and surely over you, and I would never take you back, so get that into your fucking head and sign the papers. I have been more than generous already, and you will not get another penny more. Do I make myself clear? Now, just fuck off."

With that, I ended the call. I was seething. I can't believe that I went from so happy and excited to so fucking upset. I jumped out of bed and went to the gym to try to get all this anger out of me before meeting Isabel. She didn't deserve spending the day with a miserable asshole. She needed me to be Jack.

After a hard two-hour workout, I was dead. My frustration and anger had only ebbed a bit, though. There was still a lot inside me. I needed to talk to someone, so I called Ian. The phone rang and rang, until it went to his voicemail, so I tried again. Still nothing. I thought if I saw Isabel I would be okay. She always cheered me up. Just looking at her makes my days much brighter, so I decided to go and meet her earlier, give her a surprise. I hoped it would be a good surprise and she wouldn't be upset.

I looked at myself in the mirror in my dressing room, and I thought casual would be perfect for a lunch date, so I put on my white long-sleeve Burberry shirt, a navy blue Hugo Boss jumper draped over my shoulders and knotted at my chest, a pair of dark blue jeans, and of course my navy blue Hugo Boss suede shoes. I hadn't shaved, so I had a bit of stubble. *It might come in handy*, I thought. My thoughts turned quickly, as they had lately, to Isabel. Oh God, I hoped I would be able to make them come true soon, make her scream my name. I felt a bulge building, so I turned and grabbed my keys, deciding to leave before I worked myself up too much.

I sat on my car looking to Isabel's house for a few minutes, I felt nervous, I should have called her, asked her if she would like to meet earlier, this was too early, I looked at my watch. It was 9.45 a.m. Would she be up already? Would she be upset? I took out my phone and looked at it, trying to decide if I should call her or just walk up the drive and ring the bell. I decided to just go for it. I could make an excuse or something. I got out of my car and heard music when I reached the front door. That made me stop and yet again consider whether I should have called beforehand. Now was too late, so I rang bell before I changed my mind.

"It's open," I heard Isabel shout. Was she expecting me? I looked at my wristwatch again, and it was 9.55 a.m. Only ten minutes had passed, and I was supposed to meet her at twelve, so I was way early. I just opened the front door and stepped inside slowly. The music was coming from the kitchen. It was Latin music. I knew it well; our company was a partner on the production of this particular song.

"In the kitchen, babe. Come in," Isabel said. My interest picked a bit more at the 'babe' part. Whom was she expecting? When I opened the kitchen door, the huge open-plan space was brimming with music. I halted at the site of Isabel dancing with such sexual movements. My feet would not work further. My mouth hung open, and it would not utter even a single word. She had a mop in her hand. She was wearing really short skin-tight red shorts and a tiny white top almost the size of a bra. Her short hair was tied with a thick red hair band. She was moving in such a way that I had never seen before. Don't get me wrong, I have been to a few strip clubs in the past, but no one moved like this. I was so fucking hard that it was getting painful. My jeans were not made for this.

"Come on, Lizzy dance with me, b—"

She didn't finish the sentence. She turned, and her eyes locked with mine, and she instantly froze on the spot. She blinked a few times, and I didn't even noticed my feet were moving until her lips were just inches from mine.

"W-w-what ... Jack ... how ...?"

I could not hold back any more. I grabbed her face with both my hands and crashed my lips into hers. Oh God, she tasted like fresh strawberries, sweet and juicy. I felt her hands on my hair. She was kissing me back with all the passion that I was feeling. This was even better than the dreams that had been plaguing me since I met her.

I heard someone clear their throat. It was like a bucket of cold water. I jumped and turned.

"I'm sorry. Am I interrupting something?"

Lizzy was standing in the kitchen doorway with a very amused smile on her face.

"*No*, no, Lizzy, we were just … just, you know." Isabel was trying to explain something that was as clear as day, bless her. She was so embarrassed. Her cheeks were bright red, which I found even more cute, if that was even possible.

"Yes, yes, I know. Don't stop, please. Carry on doing what I know you were doing. I'll get Mark's wallet from the cinema room and be back in a minute." Before she left, she chuckled a little and shook her head.

"Jack, what that hell are you doing here?" She sounded pissed off, but I couldn't help smiling like an asshole.

"Well, I was just in the area, and I thought, what that hell? Why not see if Isabel wants to start our date earlier. But you know what? I will swap any date for the reception I received." I couldn't stop grinning. I tasted her and I felt like a teenageboy.

"Well, well, you should've just called me, you know. I wasn't expecting you. I thought you were Lizzy." She was trying not to look into my eyes. Her arms were all over the place. It was really funny seeing her so out of control. It actually turned me on that much more. I liked that I could make her lose control, of which Isabel had plenty.

"I'm sorry. I didn't mean to upset you. Really, I didn't. What?"

She was looking at me with a deep frown on her face.

"You don't look sorry at all. Why do you keep smiling like … like … a baboon." At that, I laughed hard.

"I thought I looked good. Now you are calling me a baboon? Ouch," I said with a smirk, putting a hand on my heart. She laughed and grabbed the mop, which she had tossed to the floor. I hadn't even realized she had dropped it.

"Look, Jack, I was finishing up cleaning the floors, and I need to shower and change. It will take a little while until I get ready. If you don't mind waiting, by all means, take a seat on the living room; otherwise, you can return later." She never met my eyes again. She was nervous, I could tell.

"It's okay, I'll wait. Good things are worth the wait, believe me," I said, but I didn't move away to the living room. I just went to the kitchen doorway and leaned on it.

"Are you just going to stand there?" She looked at me this time with a shocked expression.

"Yes, Isabel, I much prefer this view to the boring one in the living room. Not that the decoration isn't beautiful there, but this one beats anything," I said, crossing my arms over my chest.

"Fine." She turned and started to mop the floors. This time she wasn't dancing; she was working fast.

"No dancing?" I asked cheekily.

"No fun when I have an audience," she said sternly.

"Oh, come on now. Surely you are used to performing. The way you were moving, girl ..." I was trying to undo her even more.

"Oh, she's not used to performing, but I keep telling her she has a real talent, this one. Dancing is in her blood, but she doesn't believe me." Lizzy was crossing the kitchen to me and smiling at Isabel.

"Shut up, Elizabeth. You're not helping," Isabel mumbled.

"Oh, I'm in trouble. She is calling me by my full name. Come on, Izzy, don't be upset. We are just playing with you," she said, looking at Isabel with a little pout.

"Yes, I know you are. You know, if you weren't already married, Lizzy, Jack here would be the perfect guy for you. You both have such a crap sense of humour," she said, looking between both of us. We all laughed out loud.

"Good thing for you I am already taken, right, Izzy?" she challenged Isabel. Isabel turned, got the mop, and passed by us completely, ignoring us both, but she had a slight grin on herlips.

"So, I gotta go. I'll see you later, guys. Have fun now. Bye bye."

Lizzy turned and left, skipping like a little kid. Isabel was putting the cleaning products away in a cabinet under the stairs.

"I like your friends. They are so much fun," I said, trying to get her to talk to me. She said nothing, which disappointed me a bit, but I gave it another shot.

"Where is Lara? I haven't seen her." She closed the door and put her hands on her hips. "Now you worry about Lara? Can you imagine if she walk into ..." She closed her eyes and then opened them again, carrying on. "If she had come in and caught us kissing, what would I have said? She would be so confused, and I wouldn't know what to tell her." She looked sad now, which in turn made me sad.

"Hey, hey, I'm sorry. I didn't think about that. I just saw you ... I didn't even realize what I was doing until I was actually doing it," I said while closing the distance between us. I put my hand on her face. She leaned into my hand, closing her eyes.

"What are we doing, Jack?" She almost whispered the question.

"I don't know, but I like it. I like it a lot," I said, wanting to kiss her again but remembering what she had said about Lara. Not wanting that to happen, I took a step back.

"So go ahead and get ready. I'll wait for you." I gave her a smile, and she smiled back at me.

"I'll be quick, okay."

"Don't worry. Just take whatever time you need. I won't go anywhere."

"In that case, I'll make you wait," she said, biting her lip and leisurely walking upstairs.

I put my hands in my back pockets and went to the living room. I was walking around looking at the picture frames that were over the fireplace and on top of the beautiful black piano. There were so many pictures—pictures of Lara when she was a baby and as she was growing. There was a beautiful picture of Isabel and Sam, her late husband, on their wedding day. They looked so happy, looking at each other with laughter. I had to pick it up to look at it closer. Life was fucked up. Isabel had lost the love of her life. Lara had lost her father at only 4 years old. It wasn't fair. I moved on to the other pictures and picked up another one. Isabel and Lara were together in this one. It was a selfie. You could tell Isabel was holding the camera. It was really, recent because Lara looked the same as she does now, missing one side tooth. They both looked so cute that my heart jumped a little. I smiled. I had feelings for Isabel, but I never thought that I would also feel for Lara, but I realized I did. I hadn't yet spent a lot of time with her, but she is so warm and sweet, and her smile is like a little sunshine—it brightens everything.

"Ready to go?" I heard Isabel say. I turned, almost dropping the picture I was holding. "Gosh, that was fast." I looked her over. She looked hot. She was wearing dark blue skinny jeans, a light pink long-sleeve shirt, and a dark pink jumper draped over her shoulders, just like I was. She had dark pink wedges, and she looked really elegant.

"Well, I had my date waiting," she said with a smile.

"Let's go then," I said, offering her my arm, which she took.

I opened the car door for her. Once she was in, I closed it. Then I went around and got in.

"So, where are you taking me this early?" It was only eleven, so I thought I'd take her to Hyde Park. I hadn't been there for a few years, and I knew that they had done works there recently. It would be nice to see what they had done. I always loved to go for walks there. It is the largest royal park, and there are always lots of exotic plants and different areas to walk in.

"Well, it's a place that I love, but I haven't been for a while now. I think it will be the perfect place," I said, looking briefly at Isabel, trying to see her reaction. She looked very relaxed and gave me a small smile.

It took longer than I thought, but London traffic is always a nightmare. I parked in one of the car parks of Hyde Park. She turned to me with surprise showing on her face. I quickly got out and went over to her side to open her door. She took my hand.

"Very smooth, Jack. Very smooth indeed." We both chuckled.

"So, I know it's a little early to have lunch, so I thought we could take a walk in the park.

Is that okay?" I asked Isabel, feeling unsure.

"It's actually a great idea. I love it here too, and I haven't been since ..." She didn't finish the sentence, just looked at her hands.

"Yeah, life sometimes takes us in different directions and make us forget the little good things." I took her hand as we walked, and she looked at our linked hands with a little smile and she blushed slightly.

"Can I ask you something?" I asked. "Sure."

"So earlier, when I caught you dancing, I noticed you were dancing in a way I've never actually seen. What was that?" I asked her.

"Well, that was Kizomba. It's a dance from Angola, a Portuguese colony. It's quite well known in Portugal, and I just love it—even though I don't think I do it right."

"Ah, I've heard of kizomba, yes, but I've never actually seen it before. You don't think you do it right? Why do you say that?"

"Well, I think Kizomba needs to be in your blood to be done correctly. It's not easy to teach your body—well, at least that's my opinion. It's hard to explain, but I think Kizomba is your sensual side mixed with African rhythm. Does that make sense?"

"Well, if the intention is to show your sensual side, then I can say you nailed it, because you were like ... wow ... I just couldn't stand there any longer without pulling you to me." She chuckled and looked at the ground, a little embarrassed.

"Can I ask you something else?" Isabel just nodded. "I know you got extremely embarrassed about our kiss—or make-out session, you could say." I chuckled, trying to keep the conversation light. "Do you regret it?" The words came out in a rush. Isabel just looked straight into my eyes.

"No, never. It's just ... it'd been so long since ... it's like I am learning everything again— how to flirt, how to interpret actions and emotions, how to date. It's so bloody hard." She was starting to move her free hand around. I had noticed when Isabel was nervous or upset, she had a habit of moving her hands and arms all over the place. It was so funny.

"Isabel, please stop trying.You are just making it harder foryourself. Don't over-think it.

That's what I am trying to do. I like you a lot. You are just this wonderful woman who I should have crossed pass with way back, but life didn't want that to happen, so I am going to pursue you now. You need to know that I will be myself, and I need to know you." She smiled again and squeezed my hand slightly. I'm not even sure she was aware of her gesture.

"I understand, and I would love to get to know you. What I have seen so far tells me a lot about you, and ... You intrigue me, Jack. But can I ask you one thing? Let's take this slow. I have Lara to think about."

"I get where you're coming from, but I'm not the 'slow' kind of guy. When I want something, I have to have it. It's not that I'm not patient, but I will not let you escape. You're too good." I stopped and took both her hands in mine and looked into her beautiful golden eyes. "Isabel, be mine. No more dating William or anyone other than me. I am asking you to give me a chance to make you happy. You want us to go slow? Fine, but don't kill me by going out with someone else, because that's what it does to me. It kills me just to know you are with another man." I was speaking to her with all the determination and passion I felt. I wanted her to see how serious I was about her. Isabel parted her lips and started to breathe faster. Her eyes moved from my eyes to my lips, but I just waited, giving her time to make up her mind. I didn't have to wait long, because she brought her lips to mine in a soft kiss.

With a little smile, she whispered, "Okay. I'll only see you, Jack. No one else. Just you." I wanted to take her right here and now, but I promised we would go slow, so I put my hand on her face and traced her lips with my thumb.

"You taste like fresh strawberries, sweet and juicy. How am I supposed to resist that when my favourite fruit is strawberries?" She laughed at that, making me smile widely.

"God, that was so cheesy."

"Welcome to getting to know me. There will be lots of cheesiness."

We both laughed. I pulled her to my side, and we walked, hugging each other, looking at the plants, and taking some pictures. I made her take a few selfies with me. I needed to have her beautiful face on my mobile. I was so happy that all the upset feelings I'd felt earlier that morning were all but forgotten.

CHAPTER 11

Isabel

I sat at the table looking at the most gorgeous eyes I had ever seen, and I couldn't for the love of God believe he wanted me. Jack declared himself. He doesn't want me to see anyone else, which of course I agreed to, because it's what I want also, but I never expected him to ask me that. He seems so sure of himself all the time, as if he has this sense of control, but then, with me ... he doesn't seem to have any control. I get butterflies in my tummy knowing that he loses control around me. I smiled thinking of this.

"What's so funny?" Jack asked.

"Nothing, nothing at all." I dismissed the thought, averting my eyes to the lunch menu. Jack took me to a little Indian restaurant not far from Hyde Park so we didn't have to take the car.

"Hello, Mr Jack, are you ready to order?" a young Indian lad asked. This restaurant seemed to be a family run business, and they knew Jack. *Interesting.*

"Hi, Raj. Can you bring my usual please?" Jack said, looking at me with a smile. "I can see you come here often."

"My mum brought me here when I was eight, and since then it's become our favourite place."

"Can I have lamb balti and mushroom fried rice with a salad on the side? Thank you." "It won't be long." The lad smiled when taking the menu from me.

"So, your mum. Were you close?"

"Yes. As you can imagine, my dad was extremely busy with building up a company and had very little time, so my mum always made sure she was there for everything. Please don't get me wrong. My dad is a fantastic father. He always made sure we had everything, but it was extremely hard to build a successful company and be present for his family outings. Both my mum and I always understood that. Maybe because he never lied, he always made sure to be on time. When he wasn't sure that he could make it, he would be honest with us, explaining the reason. I remember my parents attending a lot of events together most evenings, but before they left, they both made sure I was in bed, tucked in. Either my mum or my dad would come in and tuck me in. Sometimes both of them would, and I would be so happy and feel so lucky to have such great parents. My best friend, Ian, had an absent father—not because he was a successful businessman but because he preferred to spend time with his mistresses than his family. That saddens me eventoday."

Jack has a heart of gold. I knew this before, but hearing him speak about the love of his family and his best friend's family issues showed me what a good a man he is.

"I knew your father was a kind man, but I never had the chance to meet your mother.

She sounds wonderful."

"She was." Jack averted his eyes and gave a sad smile. "She passed away five years ago. It's still difficult sometimes. I would call her for advice or even just to hear her voice, you know. Sometimes I still have the urge to call her but it hits me that I can't."

"I know the feeling." I understood loss very well. "Anyway, so Lara, when can we discuss her?"

"I will book a meeting between us this week. Tomorrow, when I get to the office, I'll look at the schedule and fit us in. Is that okay?"

"Of course."

Our food came, and it looked amazing. Jack had the same as me, only the rice was plain whereas mine was mushroom fried rice. There was a mixed platter with small bite-size dishes. Jack said it's what he orders when he brings friends so you can try almost all their dishes. The food was amazing, and I ate until I was busting.

"Oh God, I can't eat one more bite. I'm bursting," I said, feeling like a whale. "Did you like it?" Jack said with a little chuckle.

"It was divine, but I cannot move now."

"Don't worry—I can carry you," he said, leaning in closer to me.

"Yeah right, as if you could lift me. I am heavier than I look, mister, and now that I've eaten like a whale, you definitely wouldn't be able to pick me up."

Jack leaned back in his chair. "Is that a challenge I hear?" he said, trying to keep a straight face. I bit my bottom lip, trying to keep from giggling.

"No, not a challenge, just a fact."

He laughed and shook his head slightly.

"Okay, we could always test that theory," he said, smirking.

"*No*, no, no, no." I looked around to see if anyone had heard our conversation. "I can walk on my own two legs, but thank you," I said, starting to getup.

"All right, but if you change your mind, please let me know. I will be more than happy to carry you all the way to your house." There it was again, that cheeky smile that always made me feel like jelly.

"Duly noted," I said, trying to look everywhere other than him. We walked to the car at a slow pace, chatting some more about his family and my family.

"So, you are British born and bred, but you have a cute accent. How does that happen?" he said chuckling.

"Don't ask me. That is something I always wondered. For the life of me, I can't figure that out."

When we were at the car, Jack pushed me against it and kissed me hard—with need, with so much passion. I felt my hands gripping his shirt at his chest, pulling him even closer to me. His hands were in my hair, and we were so lost in the moment that we forgot where we were, until we heard a group of teenagers giggling. One of them said something like, "Get a room." Jack stood back slightly, looking into my eyes.

"I had to do it. I have been holding out for too long. Isabel, you are like a drug to me." He caressed my cheek with his thumb. I looked at his lips. They were swollen from kissing me, and I almost lost it with the need I felt. I needed to feel those lips everywhere on me.

"As much as I want you right now, we need to go," he said, opening the door of the car for me. I was in such a daze that I didn't hear my phone until Jack pointed it out to me.

"Hello."

"Hi, Mummy. What time you picking me up from Vo?"

Oh shit, for the first time in my life, I forgot Lara was with my mum.

"Oh, sweet pea, um … I will be there in about one hour. I've just been a bit busy and didn't see the time."

"It's okay. Vo just needed to know. Also, do you want to have an early dinner here, or will we go home straight away?" I was so full I couldn't eat for the rest of the day.

"We are going straight home, sweetie. I'll order something for you later." "Okay, Mummy. We'll see you in bit then. Love you. Bye."

"Love you. Bye. Mwah." I looked at Jack, and he had a huge smile on his face. "What?" I asked, confused.

"Nothing, I just think you are so cute when you're nervous." "I'm not nervous."

"Oh, you are so."

"What? No I'm not. I was just … thinking, and … never mind." I was blushing like a bloody tomato. This only made Jack laugh out loud.

"Stop. Jack, stop." I slapped his arm lightly.

"Oh, she is getting mad now. Okay, okay, I won't laugh again." He was trying to hold his laughter, but that made me laugh.

"Now that's not fair. How come you can laugh and I can't?" he said, sounding really innocent. I just gave him a stern look, and we both laughed.

"I need to pick Lara up after you drop me at home, so I can't invite you in for a coffee."

He said something under his breath which I didn't catch, but he covered it up with "Next time, then." The way he said it left me breathless. I was sure he didn't mean *coffee* would be next time.

"Yeah, next time," I said a bit too quickly.

When Jack dropped me off at home, he kissed me again, taking my breath away. His lips knew exactly what they were doing. I was almost dragging him inside with me, but I broke up the kiss before it went too far.

"I'll see you tomorrow, Jack. Thank you for the lunch date." I wanted to thank him for the kisses too, but I would sound dumb, so I stopped myself.

"Hmmm, you really are going to make me go home now, aren't you?" He was leaning on the doorframe with a smirk, and his eyes were shining like a river when the sun hits it.

"Yes, Jack. You are a gentleman, hence why you are leaving."

"Oh, Isabel, you don't know me well enough yet. When you get to know me, you will see I am no gentleman," he said with hooded eyes, making my insides quiver.

"I'll see you tomorrow, Jack," I said, pushing him a little.

"See you tomorrow, sweet Isabel. Sleep well," he said before turning to leave. I had to close the front door quickly before I changed my mind. I was feeling so hot right now. The way he looked at me, like he wanted to devour me. And I so wanted him to devour me. God, just to feel his lips on my skin would be ...

Isabel, snap out of it. Lara. Think of Lara. You need to go and get her.

That snapped me right out.

My mum asked me a thousand questions about my date with William that I wasn't really interested in answering. In the end, I told her that it wouldn't work out because I saw him as just a friend, nothing else. She was disappointed, I could tell, but she didn't press me more.

Lara was her usual happy and carefree self. On the way back, she kept talking, telling me what she and my mum had been up to over the weekend, but I kept quiet. I just felt a sense of loss, like I was missing something. Jack was still on my mind when I lay on my bed that night. I picked up the phone, making a rash decision to text him.

Are you asleep?

Hopefully I wouldn't wake him up.

Nope, I can't stop thinking of you sweet Isabel.

My heart just stopped.

Oh yeah? What about me?

The response was immediate.

All of you, your lips, your sweet skin, how your golden eyes almost close when I come close to you, the feel of your body against mine ... I could go on and on, but if I did that, I would turn up at your door and do all of what I desire to you.

Oh my God, how was I going to reply to that?

What you desire?????

Yes, Isabel what I desire, what I want to do to you. Do you need me to spell it out?

I could see him typing and smirking that cheeky smirk of his.

No, I think I get the entire picture without you having to spell it out.

Good, but just so you know, whatever you are thinking, believe me, it's not even close to what I want to do. Soon, Isabel, soon you will understand what my desires are. Have a good night, keep thinking of me as I am thinking of you xx

This was a bad idea. I felt so hot right now that I could combust. I smiled, knowing that he was probably feeling as I did: hot and bothered. How am I going to manage to do my work this week knowing Jack is next door, the way he makes me feel? I like challenges, but this is a challenge I am afraid I might lose.

Monday came, and I was feeling so nervous, but I also couldn't wait to see his face.

"Good morning, Isabel," Jack said when he walked in.

"Good morning, Jack," I said in a small voice.

"So, I have arranged a meeting for Wednesday at 2.20 p.m. for us to go over Lara's options. The schedule is printed on your desk and also updated on your desktop. Oh, what did you think of the works. Does it look as we discussed?" I said, trying to sound as professional as possible.

"Oh, I didn't even notice. Let me put my file in my office. I will look around and speak to a few members of staff just to make sure it's all in order," he said.

Jack went around the office, and he reached my desk with a huge smile on his face. "Isabel, this is so great. I love that it's so quiet now. We can't hear a thing when we step out of the lift. That's probably why I didn't notice anything—because it was so quiet that my brain didn't process where I was. Everyone is really pleased with the changes, and I really like that this area is bigger and that you chose full glass walls as we enter this area. It doesn't feel closed off at all."

"Thank God you like it. I was a bit nervous that you might think I was closing off all the areas of this floor."

"Oh no. The glass really opens up the space. And the colour scheme is so sophisticated. Well done. Great job." He winked and went into his office. Okay, so this isn't going to be that difficult. Jack seems great at keeping professional, which helps me keep it that way.

The day went by in a blur. Jack had many meetings, and not seeing him a lot helped me concentrate on work. I picked Lara up from her music lessons. I told her about the meeting with Jack and the possibility of working with his company.

"Yes, Mummy. I like Jack. I want to work with him."

"Well, sweet pea, you have a lot of options. I think it's best that Mummy arrange meetings with other recording companies first, and then we can decide what is best for you." I knew Reeds Recordings would be the best, but I needed to give Lara other options.

"No, Mummy. I don't want to go with anyone else. Besides, Reeds Recordings is the best—Ms Rory said so."

So, she had spoken to her newest music teacher about it. "Okay, fine. If you are completely sure about this ..." "Yes, Mummy, I am sure."

"I will see what Jack offers. If I think I can negotiate, I will get the best deal." "I know you will, Mummy. Jack will do whatever you want," she said, smiling. "Whatever do you mean?" I asked.

"You know Jack likes you, so he'll do whatever you ask him. You won't have to try too hard," she said with such conviction.

"Why do you say Jack likes me?"

"Mummy, anyone can see Jack adores you. He fancies you. What? I understand it all, Mummy. I'm a big girl now." I cannot believe what my little girl was saying. Did she see something. Maybe my texts or something? I thought of every moment she could have seen us.

"Stop worrying, Mummy. It's okay. I can see you like Jack too. He is so dreamy, and he is really kind and gorgeous—and he is my friend."

I looked at her with my mouth wide open. "How old are you?" I said, looking at her.

"I'm almost nine. I told you, I'm a big girl." We both laughed. This helped a lot, knowing my daughter liked Jack. It helped me to continue with whatever we were doing.

The rest of the week went by quite fast. Jack and I had a routine going. During working hours, we spoke only about work, keeping it professional, but at the end of the day, we would text each other and even speak on the phone for quite a while. We would talk about things outside work, like his battle with his ex and Lara's newfound love of writing her own music pieces, which we both found so amazing at her age, being this talented and so focused. I also often spoke of Sam. You would have thought this would feel strange, but with Jack, it felt comfortable. He seemed so interested in knowing my past.

I spoke twice with William, the first time to let him know that I had found someone who made me happy and that I would be dating him exclusively. The second time he called to see if I would like to go for a coffee sometime, "as friends, nothing more", as he put it. I said I would like that, and perhaps Jack could come along. It would give them an opportunity to get to know each other, and we could all become friends. William said it was a great idea, but Jack didn't feel the same, even though he agreed to go with me just to make sure William "knew his place". Yes, that's actually what he said, with that cheeky smirk he gave me whenever he was full ofhimself.

Today was a really important day for Jack—Saturday, the day of the National Music Awards ceremony, which we were attending together. Jack said yesterday that we would have a great night and that he would be picking me up around 7 p.m. I put on my gown, and I had my makeup and my hair all done up. I was looking into the mirror and found myself smiling with excitement. Lara was spending the weekend with my mum again. This was the fourth weekend in a row she had spent with my mum, and I felt bad, but in all honesty, Lara loves to spend time with her grandma, and I know they are both safe that way too.

My doorbell rang, and I looked at myself once more. My gown was a flowing black sheer with golden satin underneath, with a black sheer belt tied in a bow at the back. It had a deep plunging neck that almost reached my belly button. I added a long, thin gold necklace that came up to just before the plunge and a pair of long, thin gold earrings. The clutch bag came with the dress, so it was made out of the same fabric and colours, and my shoes were Christian Louboutin golden high heels. My makeup was light and had golden shimmer eyeshadow. My hair had large curls, which made it seem even shorter but in a really glamorous way. I thought I looked good. The doorbell rang again, and I dashed downstairs. When I got to the door, I took a breath before opening it. Jack was, in a black tuxedo. Oh my, oh my, what a site. His hair was styled to one side, slicked back perfectly, but his eyes looked dark tonight. I don't know if it was the black tuxedo or what, but they looked so fucking sexy. I almost pulled him inside.

"Isabel, you look fantastic. You just took my breath away," he said, stepping closer to me in slow, measured steps.

"Jack, you don't look too bad yourself," I said in a small, breathless voice that I couldn't recognize. He was so close now that our noses were almost touching. Then, in a quick movement, Jack had me against my front door, encasing me there with his lips on mine. He let out a loud moan.

"Shit, Isabel, what are you doing to me?" Jack said, resting his forehead on mine and breathing hard. "I can't keep control with you." He closed his eyes and then stepped back a little. He shoved his hands in his pockets, and I cleared my throat.

"Well, that was ... a nice greeting," I said, smiling. "Just give me a second. I need to reapply my lipstick."

"I wouldn't do that just yet. You know, the ride there is still about twenty minutes," he said with a smirk.

"Yeah? Well, I am taking my lipstick with me," I said, returning his smirk.

"Oh, by the way, your face has my lipstick all over it," I said, passing by him and chucking.

"Haha, funny."

"No, I'm serious." I was laughing now because the look on his face was so funny. "Shit," he said when he looked at himself in the limo's mirror. The driver was waiting with the limo's door open so both Jack and I could go in. "This is bloody posh," I said under my breath.

"What was that?"

"Oh, nothing. Did you hire this for us today?"

"No, this is one of my dad's. He has two of these. I used to ride in one when I was in school. It used to be my school transportation."

"Wow, rich boy. Don't tell me you had a personal bodyguard too," I said with amusement.

"Go ahead, laugh. My parents are rich, and yes, I am rich, but I only use a limo for events like these—you know that. I like to drive myself, but these events expect this sort of thing. You don't mind, do you?" He looked worried.

"What, being escorted by a handsome fella in a limo to an awards ceremony? Don't be daft. This is wonderful," I said.

"Good, I thought for a moment there you would kick me to the curb." We both smiled. Jack took my hand and kissed it ever so gently. I couldn't understand him. One moment he was this out-of-control man, kissing me passionately, grabbing me in such a demanding way, and in the next he was this calm gentleman. It was confusing the hell out of me.

I was expecting photographers as this was a red-carpet event, but holy hell, I did not expect to see this many. The events I used to attend with Sam were big, but this? This was another level. From the moment we stepped foot outside the limo, there was a huge buzz. We were constantly being asked if we were together. Did Mrs Reed know we were attending together? God, this was going to come and bite our asses. I should never have accepted the invitation to come, even if it was as Jack's PA. These bloody photographers would find out we were seeing each other, and it would all go to shit for his divorce case.

Jack was so cool and collected. He answered a few questions.

"This is Ms Winter. She is my PA, and this is not a date. Ms Winter is here to assist me on a purely professional basis." When he said this, I felt myself relax a bit. I smiled, and we started to move forward.

"Jack, I don't think this was a good idea."

"What? To be escorted by a gorgeous fella in a limo to an award ceremony?" He chuckled. "Stop worrying. You will see a few people bring their PAs with them. This is an ideal place to do business, actually. And as I planned, we are here to do business, so you are where you should be," he said. He wiggled his eyebrows, which made me laugh.

The gala was beautifully decorated, with huge chandeliers hanging from the ceiling, red velvet chairs, and huge flower arrangements all around—a really sophisticated look. I was so nervous. People kept looking our way, and many of them came to talk to Jack. Of course, I always stayed a step back and only addressed someone when I was addressed, or when Jack requested my input. I think I was doing what I was supposed to be doing as a PA; I even took notes on my mobile. We were escorted to our seat before the ceremony started. Jack grabbed my hand, and I immediately withdraw, shaking my head. Jack must have noticed the panic in my eyes, because he turned his eyes away and let me take my seat without a word. I started to look around to see if anyone had noticed, and I didn't see anyone looking our way, so I assumed no one had seen our exchange. That was arelief.

The award ceremony went really well, and I kept taking notes on my mobile. On Monday, I would run a few things by Jack that I'd noticed, which would perhaps help him strike a deal or two.

When the ceremony was over, everyone was ushered to a party room, where there was a stage, tables and chairs for dining, and a huge TV screen. We were taken to a table by a staff member, and I was quite pleased that I knew most of them. There was Mr Reed, Jack's dad, Mr and Mrs Smith, and Mr and Mrs Lanes, a sweet old couple born from old money but who weren't snobs; they were so kind, and I knew them from previous events I used to attend with Sam. Mr Lanes had business with all sorts of sports, and they were among Sam's sponsors.

When they saw me, Mrs Lanes got up and hugged me tightly.

"Isabel, my dear Isabel, how nice to see you here, darling. How are you? Oh God, you are even more stunning—if that is even possible."

"Oh, Mrs Lanes, thank you. You are too kind. It's really nice to see you. It has been a long time."

"Too long indeed, my dear. Michelle is right—you are stunning." Mr Lanes was holding onto both my hands.

"I see you know each other," Jack said from behind me.

"Oh, I'm sorry, Jack. Yes, we have known each other for over eight years now. Mr and Mrs Lanes, I am Jack's PA at Reeds Recordings."

"Charles, your son, has turned into a fine young man indeed. Very handsome, but of course, with a mother as beautiful as his, he couldn't be anything other than gorgeous," Mrs Lanes said. We all laughed, and Jack actually blushed.

"Yes, Michelle. He does resemble his mother a lot—thank God for that." Mr Reed said. We went around the table, kissing and shaking hands. I noticed there was an empty seat at the other side of Jack and was about to ask if he knew who the seat was for.

"Jack, baby, you're finally here." Everyone stopped chatting and looked to the source of the squeaky voice. The newcomer had really long, very blond, almost white, hair. She was very tall with the high heels she was wearing. She was definitely Jack's height, and Jack is really, really tall, standing about six foot five. She was beautiful and sexy, in a tight blood-red dress—if you could call it a dress; you could see her nipples through the bloody thing—and her middle was all showing, with a slit at the front that didn't leave anything to the imagination. She was looking me up and down, just as I was doing it to her.

"What are you doing here, Jessica?" Jack said, standing up so fast that he almost dragged the tablecloth with him.

"Oh, Jack, you knew I would be here. How could I not? I know half the people here—and you *are* my husband."

"Not for long we're not. Jessica, we've been separated for over eight months—everyone knows that—so you don't have to act any longer. Why don't you just leave?" He was so mad. I had never seen him like this. He was speaking quietly but in such a mean, hard voice that my heart stopped. Who was this man?

"Jack, don't be ridiculous. I will never leave. I have the same right as you to be here in this circle. Oh, what do we have here? Jack, are you cheating on me?"

"What the fuck?" Jack said, looking at her as if she'd gone mad. To be honest, she did look like she was on something, speaking as if they were still living together.

"Jessica, are you drunk or on drugs? Because that is the only reason I see for you to be behaving like this. Stop this act. We are not a couple."

"Jack, I think I'd better go," I said to Jack gently, not wanting them to create a scene. "No, Isabel. You are here working. If someone should leave, it should definitely be Jessica," said Mr Reed. I was so surprised he said something that I couldn't answer.

"My father is right, Isabel. You are not leaving, but Jessica will be, and if she doesn't, then at least she will be seated at a different table." Jack turned and left us to go and sort the seating issue.

"Well, Isabel, is it? Don't get too comfortable. It won't last long, love. Ladies and gentlemen, enjoy this pleasant evening, because I surely will." With that, she walked away, swaying her hips a little too much.

"Don't take any notice of that miserable women. She never deserved Jack." Mrs Lanes said, patting my hand.

"Michelle is right, dear. Don't take any notice," Mr Reed said, giving me a small smile. I just nodded politely, but I felt bad. I'd just met the women who'd had Jack's heart, and I couldn't for the life of me understand how he could have loved such a deluded creature.

When Jack returned to the table, he didn't look at me. In fact, all night, he was quiet and withdrawn. I would occasionally catch him looking my way, and when I tried to catch his eye, he would cast down his gaze, as if he were ashamed. This made me sad. I wanted to see his smile, his cheeky grin, his beautiful green eyes shine, so, in an impulse, I grabbed his hand and stood up.

"Come dance with me, Jack." He looked at me for the first time since the incident with his ex.

"Isabel, I don't think is a good idea." Jack looked so sad, which made me even more determined. I bent down slightly, coming closer to him.

"Jack, I am asking you to dance with me, and you *will* dance with me, even if I have to drag you to the bloody dance floor. I am giving you a chance to come nicely without causing a terrible scene." I gave him my best stern look.

"You wouldn't dare. I am your boss, after all. I could just fire you."

I could see his cheeky smirk starting to emerge from the corners of his lips. I stood straighter, dropped his hand, and put it on my hip.

"You won't fire me because I am a damn good PA. Now stop stalling and get your butt out of that chair and dance with me." I heard someone laugh out loud. I wasn't expecting it to be Mr Reed.

"Well, son, what you waiting for?" Jack just smiled and got up.

"May I have this dance milady?" He bowed down low with his hand extended. I took his hand, laughing. On our way to the dance floor, I noticed a few heads turning our way.

Oh, God, what am I doing?

We started dancing, and I was so surprised how great of a dancer Jack was. He had full control, very smooth. What made my heart race wasn't the dance moves he had, though. It was his hand resting at the base of my back. I felt his heat coming from it, and when he pulled me even closer to him, I looked up into those eyes that made me want to do things, things that I hadn't done in so fucking long.

"You are so beautiful," he said, looking at me, his eyes closing slightly. "Mmm."

It was all I could manage—just a little moan.

I forgot how to speak, how to breathe, where I was, and in fact who I was. The music changed to a faster ballroom dance, and we got into it so naturally. Jack spun me around this way and that way, and I kept the pace. At the end of the music, Jack dipped me low, keeping his face so close to mine that all I could see were his green eyes.

"Let's get out of here," Jack whispered, and I heard loud applause. We both stood up straight, and everyone was applauding us. Yes, us. Apparently, we were the centre of all the attention, including someone whose attention I'd rather not get: Jessica, Jack's ex-wife. She was looking at us with a triumphant smirk and her mobile in her hand.

"Jack, we really need to leave." He turned his attention to where I was looking, and he looked at me with a serious expression.

"Yes, we do."

Without another word, we got our things from the table, and with a quick goodbye to everyone, we left. My heart was in my mouth. I was sure he would be in trouble with the divorce proceedings. Jessica now had something against Jack, and I was worried for him. When we were in our limo, I grabbed Jack's hand.

"Jack, I am so very sorry. I shouldn't have come." He spun to look at me.

"What? Why are you sorry? You haven't done anything wrong. *We* haven't done anything wrong."

"Jessica has been recording everything. Surely you must be worried how it will affect the divorce case?" I couldn't believe how relaxed Jack seemed. Moments ago I saw the dislike on his face, and now he didn't seem worried atall.

"Isabel, she has nothing. We've been separated over eight months, and what she has on video is us dancing very well. Don't stress yourself with Jessica. She has no choice but to sign the papers. My solicitor has everything under control. Our plan A didn't work, but plan B will hit her like a bulldozer," he said, smiling. He brought his thumb to my cheek.

"But you were worried when you noticed she was filming. I saw the look in your face." "I wasn't worried at all. I was upset because she is still playing games, which I hate.

Really, Isabel, all is well—I promise."

Without another word, he kissed me. Not a slow kiss, either. This was ... well, like lava. Before I knew it, I was on his lap, his hands on my hips and my hands, well ... trying to take his bow tie off. I say trying because I was having trouble taking it off. I clearly was so out of practice it was pathetic, really. Jack was kissing me on my neck when he realized what I was trying to do. I felt his smile.

"Isabel, we not too far from home. What I want to do to you would be better at home, where there won't be anyone around." That woke me up from the daze I was in. Shit, did I really throw myself at him. How fucking desperate I am. I brought my forehead to his, and we were both panting, as if we had been running for miles. God, I needed him so badly that my heart could not return to its normal rhythm. I sat beside him, and he planted small, gentle kisses on my face. We were quiet until we arrived at my house. The limo came to a stop, and the driver opened the door for Jack. He came around to open my door. In just that small instant, my thoughts were all jumbled up together. I wanted him so badly, but I was so scared— scared for what would happen to our newfound relationship, scared that my feelings would change, scared that his feelings for me would change. When Jack opened the door for me and I stepped out, he looked into my eyes for a little while. Then he smiled and kissed my lips so lightly that I almost didn't feel it.

"Isabel, I don't have to come in or do anything you don't want to or not ready for."

He looked so genuine. I could see in his beautiful green eyes that he meant every word. In that instant, I saw what I wanted, and all my fears left me. I grabbed his hand and pulled him towards the house. Jack kept quiet. I opened the front door and pulled him inside with such force, closing the door so fast. I never knew I could do such thing. I pushed him against the door. I kissed him. Jack responded with so much heat, grabbing my dress, riding it up, and grabbing my ass. I quickly laced my legs around his waist. He started to climb the stairs, never taking his mouth off mine, and his hands were kneading my ass, making my sex clench in anticipation.

"Last door on the right," I managed to say. I didn't even know how I managed to utter the worlds. I felt I was in another world. His smell, his taste, made me so delirious. I hadn't been touched this way in so long that I almost came just feeling his hardness rubbing in my sex as he walked. He threw the door of my bedroom back and put me down against the wall. He took a step back, looking at me, taking off his bow tie so damn slowly it was agonizing.

"Isabel, you are so fucking beautiful. Are you sure you want this? Because if I start, I won't be able to stop—not even if you beg me to." He didn't move an inch while he said this. I just nodded.

"I need to hear it, Isabel. Say it," he said in a stern voice that made me answer at once. "Yes, I want you. All of you," I said. Jack started to unbutton his shirt. He didn't even bother taking his jacket off first. When he took off both jacket and shirt and I saw his firm abs, his puffed-up chest—a total sculpture in front of me—I took an involuntary breath.

CHAPTER 12

Jack

All I wanted to hear from Isabel's lips was that she was mine and I would have her forever, no matter what.

"Turn around for me," I said gently. She didn't hesitate, which turned me on even more if that was even possible. My dick was so hard that it was actually painful. I started to kiss her neck, then her shoulder, all the while unzipping her dress. Slowly I pulled her dress down, past her breasts and her hips, until it hit the floor. Isabel was breathing so fast that I worried she would faint.

"Breathe, baby. Just breathe. I'll be gentle and will take it slow," I said, trying to get her to relax but feeling as though I couldn't take it slow at all. I had to be gentle. I couldn't let my lust make me lose control. I needed to be in control with her. She was my glass piece, so very breakable even though she was so tough. She was like glass, very fragile. I explored her body with my hands. My mouth was also going where my hands go, from her neck to her shoulder, to her back to her hips. I turned her to face me and kissed her lips, stepping forward until the back of her legs hit the bed. Isabel sat on the bed and crawled backwards further into the bed. I stood there looking at her in her one-piece black lace lingerie. I took off my trousers and socks, leaving my boxers on. I needed to wait for the right time. She needed to get used to this, and by the look on her face, she was intimidated by my size. I didn't want her to be scared, so I had to take it slow. I grabbed her leg and started to kiss upwards, planting a kiss on her pussybriefly.

She moaned loudly and I smiled slightly, pleased that I was making her crazy with need. She grabbed my head, but I carried on up taking her lingerie off slowly. I kissed her breasts, licking and sucking on her nipples, making her pant and moan all over again. God, this was so fucking hard to control. When she moaned, it made my dick twitch continuously.

"Oh, Jack ..."

Fuck, my name on her lips was delirious. "What do you want, Isabel?"

She just moaned loudly. I moved down, kissing every inch of her stomach. Reaching her pussy, I licked and sucked while kneading her nipples with my hands until she reached an orgasm so intense that in that moment I saw how badly she needed this. It felt so good knowing it was me who brought her this relief. I kissed her lips and her neck once more, with my finger working her clit from slow to a much faster rhythm. She arched her back, and I took my boxers off. She grabbed my ass closer to her.

"What do you want, Isabel?" She once again moaned, but this time I didn't move. I waited for her to tell me what she wanted.

"Jack ..."

"Yes, tell me. Tell me what you want. I need you to say it out loud, baby." "You."

"I'm here."

"You inside me."

"Still don't know what you want." I needed her to tell me. "Fuck me, Jack, now."

I didn't wait any longer. I opened her legs and slowly entered her. She was so tight. God, how was this possible? She had a child, and yet she was so tight and was so hot. I didn't know how long I could last. I started slowly but soon lost control and was slamming into her so fast.

She was panting and moaning. I felt her tightening around my shaft, and I couldn't take it any longer, so I came too with such force that I growled.

We were both panting. I was holding her against my chest. I couldn't believe how good this was, how good I felt, how right this was.

"God this was … wow," Isabel said.

"Sorry, baby, but I'm not God. You certainly got my name wrong," I said, joking with her.

She swatted me on the chest and chuckled.

"Now seriously, you okay? I didn't hurt you, did I?" I asked.

"I'm more than okay. I'm great. You were great. Thank you," she said. Then she started to kiss me again, which of course I reciprocated. Isabel climbed into my lap while kissing me.

"Are you sure you want another go, because this time I will take my time with you, sweet Isabel."

"Oh, yeah. Maybe you might not be able to control yourself, Mr Reed."

"Are you challenging me, dear Isabel? Because if you are, game on." She chuckled, and I grabbed her by her hips and turned her over.

"Don't move an inch. Do you understand?" I whispered in her ear. Isabel nodded to let me know she understood. I grabbed her dress from the floor and took off the belt it had. For what I wanted to do, the size was perfect. I climbed onto the bed again.

"Bring your hands behind your back for me, baby." She tried to look back, and I put my hand on her back.

"Isabel, do you trust me?" I whispered again into her ear, planting a small kiss on it. "Yes."

"I want to please you, and I will show you what real pleasure is. Bring your hands behind your back." This time she complied. I grabbed both her feet and tied one end of the sheer belt to both her ankles. Then I tied the other end to both her wrists.

"Jack, what're you doing?" I stood back on my knees, looking at Isabel, trying to turn so she could see me. I started to plant kisses on her feet and her legs. Then I lifted her ass and propped her on her knees, her face on the bed with her ass and pussy in full view—the perfect position to pleasure her.

"Jack, what are you doing?" Isabel asked again, and again I didn't answer. I started to kiss her neck and her back while playing with her nipples with my thumbs. Isabel moaned and took fast and loud intakes of air.

"I, sweet Isabel, already told you what I am going to do," I said. I trailed my tongue from the top of her back to her ass, and Isabel started to pull on the bonds.

"Jack, no. What are you doing?"

"Shhhh, don't struggle. This will be for your pleasure. I am going to show you what I am good at."

"I already know what you are good at," she said breathlessly, which made me smile. "Oh, sweet Isabel, you haven't seen anything yet." I started to kiss her bottom cheeks, moving very slowly downward, coming to her clit. I started to taste her. She was already so very ready for me, but this time I would take my time, even though my shaft was so hard and bobbing on its own. It didn't take long for Isabel climax, but I didn't stop. I started on her ass with my finger, bringing her juices from her pussy to her asshole, lubricating it. She, of course, started to struggle against her bonds again. I got the impression this was her first time experiencing this. That thought alone made me want to enter her immediately, but I had to pause myself.

"Jack, I never ..."

Yep, just like I thought. This ass had never had the pleasure it deserves.

"Do you want me to stop?" I needed to make sure I wasn't going To Fast. Isabel didn't answer—she just moaned. This was the reaction I was after, but still I thought I had better take it easy.

"I won't enter you tonight. Tonight I will only play a little. We have time, baby. I'll take it slow with you." Well, as slow as I could control, I thought. I was tasting her again while fingering her butt. She was moaning so loudly now that I almost lost myself on the sound. She came once more, shouting my name a couple of times. I took of her bonds and turned her over, kissing her wrists, arm, shoulder, neck, and lips. She kissed me back with so much passion, I was actually shocked and impressed that she had such stamina.

"God, Isabel, you are so fucking hot. I can't hold it any longer, baby."

"So don't. I want you, Jack. I need you inside me." I didn't wait. I lifted her leg up and took her deep, losing myself on her moist sex, which was soaking from her previous few climaxes. I licked and sucked on her nipples and moved in such a way that my pubic bone was rubbing her clit. I was so overwhelmed with her feeling, her taste, her smell, and her loud moans that I let myself go. Isabel found her release too. We were both panting so loudly, lying side by side, looking up at the ceiling.

"Still want more?" I said, smiling.

"God no. I think if I come one more time, I'll die. This was amazing. I mean, I never tried ... you know, the ... the ass thing, but it was ... quite pleasurable."

"I aim to please," I said, grinning. Isabel laughed. We were so exhausted that we fell asleep almost instantly. I hadn't slept that well in so long that when I woke up the next day, on an empty bed, I looked at my wristwatch and was shocked to find it was 11.30 a.m. I had to look again just to make sure I wasn't seeing things. I got up and noticed my clothes weren't there, so I went into theen-suite-bathroomand decidedto take a quick shower. Isabel had impeccable taste and was very neat. Everything was in its place. The towels were perfectly placed on a towel warmer, the sink was shining, and it had moisturizer and hand soap on the side. I could see she takes pride in organization not just at work but at home too. I took a quick shower and wrapped towel around my middle, as I didn't have anything to change into. When I came into the bedroom, I decided to look for Isabel. I followed my nose. I could smell bacon or sausages. As I came downstairs, I heard music playing quietly. I think it was Portuguese because the beat sounded like it. As I opened the kitchen door, I spotted Isabel setting the table with so many dishes that I wondered how long she had beenup.

"Oh, good, you're up. I was going to get you." I smiled and stepped behind her and took her in my arms, squeezing her a little. I planted a kiss on her neck.

"Good morning, beautiful." She giggled and turned in my arms to face me. "Good morning. How did you sleep?"

"Good, great actually. I haven't slept like this for ... God, months." I kissed her lips gently, tracing them with my tongue. "Hmmm, breakfast never tasted so sweet," I whispered.

"Oh yeah, you haven't tried my breakfast yet. You will change opinion soon," she said with a smirk, leaving me to bring the last bits to the table. "Have a seat and dig in. Go on."

I sat and didn't know where to start.

"Isabel, how long have you been in the kitchen? Jesus you cooked enough for all of London."

"Well, after the calories we burnt, we need to recharge," she said playfully.

"Well then, you won't be leaving the kitchen, because after breakfast we will kill many more," I said, making her laugh.

"Just eat, will you?" she said, starting to fill her plate. I've never seen a woman so small eat so much food. I kept quiet because I didn't want to make her uncomfortable. Normally women don't like men commenting on what they eat.

"It's okay. You can say it, Jack. I eat like a pig." That made me drop my fork.

"No, no, not at all. I am just wondering where you put that food. I have seen you eat before, and I can say I've never seen a woman so small eat this much, but I love it. It's nice to see you enjoy food. Nowadays, women tend to eat like rabbits—only greens and two or three mouthfuls. This is nice for a change." Isabel chuckled.

"Well, I do love salad, but not on its own. For me, it has to be as a side dish to a nice plateful of real food—you know, a nice steak or chicken with rice, something like that."

I smiled at that.

After our late breakfast, we tidied up together. My clothes arrived all cleaned and pressed from the dry cleaners.

"You sent my clothes to the dry cleaners?"

"Sonia, my cleaner, took them for me this morning."

"Oh, so you do have a cleaner. I was wondering about that. Everything is so spotless and so tidy."

"Yes, I have a lady come in every day to help keep everything tidy and clean, but to be honest, Lara and I we are quite good at keeping everything in order. But the house is so big, so Sofia comes in a couple of hours a day. It just helps, you know."

"So she took them in the morning, but how did they deliver them back to you so fast?" She smiled. "I might know the owners."

"Okay, that makes more sense now. Isabel, you are a wonder, do you know that?"

"Oh yeah, do you want to find out how much of a wonder I am?" she said, grabbing my towel and dropping it to the floor. I liked this side of her—cheeky and sexy. It made me instantly hard.

"Oh, I will find out every bit of wonder you are, baby."

With that, I grabbed her ass and lifted her. Isabel didn't hesitate. She clasped her legs around my hips. Just the feeling of her against my hard shaft made me want to take her here and now, but I dragged her to the living room and laid her gently on the sofa. I noticed a vase on the corner with large black fluffy feathers and silver glitter flowers as decoration, and my brain shot straight to the feathers with an idea. I got up and headed straight to the vase.

"Jack, what is it? You okay?" Isabel was starting to get up.

"Don't move baby. Just lie down," I said, grabbing one of the large feathers. "Close your eyes for me," I said before turning to her. When I was beside her, I kneeled and kissed her lips gently and then moved my mouth to her ear.

"Keep your eyes shut and don't move. If you move, I won't give you what you want. Do you understand?"

She nodded.

"Do you understand?" I asked again, more seriously. "Yes," she whispered.

"That's better," I said, smirking. I started to strip off her summer dress very slowly, keeping my touch soft and slow. I watched her closely. I saw how her lips parted, and little moans escaped them when my hands grazed her skin. Her back arched when my hands touched her sides above her hips. Her eyes were dancing behind closed lids, and her breath came in pants, making her full chest heave in quick succession. Isabel is a beautiful woman, but like this, in this state of complete vulnerability, giving herself all to me, trusting me, she looked like an angel, an angel that was now mine. I played with the feather, bringing it from her feet up to her sex. Isabel moaned louder, and I could tell she wanted to move, but she held on. I moved up to her breasts and tickled her nipples. She clenched her hands into fists at her sides. It was so hot to see her this way. The sounds that came out of her made me so hard.

"God, Isabel, you are so hot," I whispered near her ear. That made her turn, and I kissed her lips. I dropped the feather and started to kiss her neck and play with her nipples.

"Oh, God," she moaned. She grabbed my ass, and I picked her up and sat her on my erection, diving inside her with such force that we both moaned out loud. She rode me hard, kissing me. My hands were all over her. We fucked like we were starving for one another. She came hard, shouting a little too loudly, and I couldn't hold on any longer. Feeling her spasms brought my release hard.

We lay down on the sofa, and when our breathing had steadied, I asked her, "What time do you have to pick up Lara?"

"Around 4 p.m."

"I don't know how I will let you go. This weekend has been ... exceptional." "Ditto. You only have to wait another five days."

"Yeah *only* five days. God, I don't think I will be able to work with you just outside my office door."

At this, she sat up.

"Jack, if you think you can't do this, transfer me to another department. I don't want this to get in the way of my career," she said, worry etched on her face.

"*No*, no, I'll manage. I need you to work for me. You are fantastic at what you do, and I will cope. Don't worry, okay?" I said in a rush.

"If you're sure." "Yes, I'm sure."

She smiled at me, and we kissed.

My apartment felt so empty when I arrived home. I put on some music and called Ian.

He picked up on the second ring.

"Jack, where have you been, mate? Is not like you not to call for drinks." I smiled, remembering my weekend.

"Well, my friend, let me tell you, I had the best weekend of my life."

"I heard you had a lovely time with Isabel at the music awards. I'll bet you had an even better time afterwards," he said with an amused tone.

"You got that right. I knew she was amazing, but ... she is fucking amazing." Ian chuckled.

"So, the wait and the chase was worth it, I take it." I let out a breath.

"Yeah. One thing I am sure of: I am totally in love with her, and it scares the hell out of me. I mean, she is too good, and I'm so scared I'll mess it up and end up losing her, you know?"

Ian laughed.

"Shit, you are so over heels for her. I've never seen you like this, not even when you married Jessica."

We were both quiet as I thought about his statement. He was right. I have loved Jessica, but it was different from how I felt for Isabel. My feelings for Isabel were so easy and came so fast—it was like she was made for me and only me. I feel a pain in my chest when I'm not with her, and I see things differently when I'm with her. I know this sounds really, really cheesy, but it's exactly how I feel. I'm normally in control of my emotions and situations. Hence the reason I was the best student and my father trusted me with the company. He knows I keep my control in the worst situations. But Isabel just makes me lose control. Just one look her way and I forget everything. It's not just her hot body or her beautiful golden eyes or gorgeous face. It is something more, like her soul that calls to me.

"You are right. This is different, Ian. She is mine, and I will make sure it stays that way." "Good for you, mate. Now, let's meet for a drink tomorrow after work."

"Sure, at WAX?"

"I'll call the office to let you know the time. Is that okay?" "Yeah. See you tomorrow then."

"See ya."

I looked at my watch. It was still too early to go to bed, so I went to the rooftop swimming pool for a few laps.

The week went by slowly. I was so frustrated by Friday morning that I just wanted to ditch work and take Isabel away for the weekend, but I wanted Lara to come too. When I arrived at the office, Isabel wasn't at her desk yet, so I left her a note requesting her in my office. When I heard a knock on my door, I smiled.

"Come in." I got up and was surprised to find my father, not Isabel, standing there. "Hi, son. Can we have chat?"

"Yes, of course. Come in." I gestured to the sofa, and he took a seat opposite mine. I waited for him to start, but he was just looking at me. I furrowed my brow.

"What's wrong?"

He smiled, pursing his lips.

"I was waiting for you to come to me and talk about it, but you haven't, so I'm here.

Isabel."

That's what it was about. I fidgeted a bit in my seat.

"What about Isabel?" I asked, trying to sound cool and collected; however, even talking about her made my control slip. My father, who knows me so well, chuckled and shook his head slightly.

"Jack, we both know you're attracted to her, and from what I've seen so far, she likes you." I rested back into the sofa and let out a breath.

"Okay. I don't want you to get upset about this, but ... Isabel and I are dating. I know, I know. You don't have to say it. We are careful, keeping our professional lives completely separate. When we are at work, we work hard, and it's like we don't know each other's personal lives, so you don't have to worry."

My father dropped his smile and rested his elbows on his knees.

"Son, I know you're both careful. I have been observing, and I've had Claire keep an eye out too. I know, but I needed to make sure. What I'm trying to say is that I'm not worried about how this relationship will affect the company because I know you well enough to know you would never let anything affect business. What I'm worried about is you, son. You are still in the middle of an awful divorce, and Jessica clearly wants to damage your image. You've seen that little video posted of you and Isabel last Saturday at the awards. This could get out of hand, and I worry for you, my boy," he said, worry clearly written on his face.

I got up and faced the glass overlooking the city, putting my hands on my pockets. The frustration I felt this week wasn't only because I couldn't spend any time with Isabel but also because of Jessica's stunt. She was trying to paint me as a playboy in the media so she could get more money out of the divorce.

"I know, Dad. I just can't stop living because of Jessica, you know. This is bullshit. She was the one who did wrong by me, and now she's trying to ruin my reputation. How fitting."

"Son, you never once asked for my help on this, and I am so very proud that you've dealt with everything so well, but you know I'm here and I can help."

I turned to him.

"What do you mean you can help?"

"Let my solicitors meet with yours. They'll bring Jessica down so fast she won't even get a chance to blink."

"No, Dad. I don't want to bring her down. I just need her to sign the bloody papers so I can actually start living my life. At the moment, I can't move in with someone. I need to watch whom I go out with and where. It's just ..."

"If you want to live your life, let me help. Speak to my legal team, son, please. I want to see you smile like I saw you do on Saturday. Only a blind man can't see Isabel makes you happy. She is an amazing—headstrong, clever, and gorgeous—so if you don't want to lose her, do what I ask and speak to my legal team."

I thought for a moment, closing my eyes.

"Fine. I'll try it your way and speak to them. Thank you." My father came closer to me and put his hand on my shoulder.

"Good. Now that I've done my good deed for the year, let's talk about our newest artist, Isabel's little girl." I smiled, shaking my head.

"You do know all, don't you, Dad?"

"You bet I do. Just because I'm an old man doesn't mean I don't know what's going on around here. Now, I have heard great things about this little firecracker. She has impressed our main studio, and everyone wants to work with her."

"Yes, I know. I actually secured a recording session with a few other artists and one of our songwriters. I think she has talent there too."

"You did good, son. I'm so proud of you. Since you came into the company, it has been great. Everyone is working hard to achieve your vision on all fronts."

"Thanks, Dad. That means a lot coming from you."

I walked my father to the door. When he was out of my office, he looked at Isabel. "Hi, Isabel. How are you?" She smiled that beautiful smile that lit up the whole room. "I'm great, Mr Reed. How about yourself, sir?" My father looked back at me and smirked.

"I'm great. I'm great now." He winked at me and left smiling. I cleared my throat.

"Can I see you in my office please?" I kept my voice serious. Isabel got up, dropping her smile and followed me in.

"Have a sit, Isabel, please." She did, crossing her long, slim, mouth-watering legs. I forgot to breathe again. Shit, what this woman does to me is unbelievable. I had an instant hard-on. Another frustration I had been coping with this week was getting so many of them and not being able to feast on this beauty.

"Jack, you are staring," she said, smirking a little. "Sorry." I cleared my throat.

"This is not business. I just needed to talk to you." "Okay."

"So, you know my divorce hasn't been finalized. Jessica is being difficult, and—"

"Jack, stop. Look, I know what you're going to say. It's fine. This is not working, and the timing is not right, so I'll save you from having to say it, okay? You're my boss, and we'll keep it that way nothing else."

I was shocked. My mouth was opening and closing like that of a fish, trying to speak, but my brain couldn't process what she had just said.

Okay, now I see. She thinks I don't want to date her. Shit.

"*No.* Isabel, you're wrong—God, so wrong. That's not it at all. I don't want to stop dating you. Per the contrary, I wanted to make it official and ask you to become my girlfriend. Even though I'm not divorced yet and I won't be able to live freely, I want only you. I need you to be with me as my girlfriend." She blinked a few times in quick succession.

"Oh." She furrowed her brow but didn't speak.

"Isabel, say something, please. I just can't take it not being able to call you my girlfriend every time anyone close to me asks about you—like my Dad or Ian. But if you are not there yet, then I understand. I promised we would take it slow, so I'll just have to deal with it."

She smiled.

"No, Jack. I was just expecting you to stop seeing me because of all this trouble in the media about our video and all."

"Isabel, I told you not to worry about Jessica. I am dealing with her. Besides, my reputation won't be damaged because of one dance."

"I just don't want to create any difficulties in the case, you know."

"You're not, baby," I said, getting up and coming around the desk, crouching near her. "Isabel, I've never met anyone like you. I cannot let you go, not now not ever," I said, looking deep into her golden eyes. Not waiting for her to answer, I kissed her lips passionately. "This morning I wanted to ditch work and take you and Lara away somewhere."

"And now?" she asked.

"Even more so. Please, let's do this. I'll get Calvin to cover for us." "No," she answered. I got up and sat on my desk opposite her. "What do you mean no?"

She smiled. "Do you need a definition for no, Mr Junior Reed."

"What I need is you and me right now right here, but I know that can't happen, so I asked you to go away with me and Lara so we can start our girlfriend-and-boyfriend thing."

Isabel got up really slowly and put both her hands on the desk on each side of me, coming closer to my face.

"I haven't actually agreed to be your girlfriend yet. And besides, I never ditch work, sir, not even for the boss. Now, you are going to look at the files I left on your desk and sign them as per my previous request while I go on with my daily tasks. I finish at 5.30 p.m. today, Mr Junior Reed. That is when I leave my job, not any earlier, so if you will excuse me, I have a lot of work to do." She spoke so slowly, looking me in the eye, not letting my gaze wander. She was seduction on heels. Fuck, I wanted her on my desk right now, but she turned around so fast, closing the door behind her, that I was left breathless and so fucking hard I had to close my eyes and hold onto the desk to control my instinct to bolt out of the door and drag her back into the office and do what I really wanted to do withher.

"Fuck, she is going to kill me like this," I whispered to myself.

I kept checking my watch. Every time Isabel called me to put someone through, I would feel a twitch in my trousers. This was getting ridiculous. At 5.25 p.m., I closed the laptop and switched off the desktop. I got up and rushed out of the office.

"Time to go, Isabel," I said impatiently. She looked at her wristwatch. "Nope, still two minutes." She was full on smirking now.

"What? Not on my watch. That's it—you're finished for the day."

She smiled, getting up and very slowly gathering her things, making sure everything was in place.

"Oh, come on. Now, you're taking the mick," I said, tapping my foot.

"Relax, Jack. The day hasn't finished yet," she said, passing by me with smooth steps. "No, it hasn't, but it has been a fucking long day," I whispered.

"Did you say something?"

"No, nothing at all, Ms Winter," I said, walking to the lift as quickly as possible. When the lift arrived, there were a few people inside. I moved to one side so Isabel could come in and stand in front of me. She eyed me suspiciously, and I smirked a little. Once she had turned her back to me, I looked at the other people. Everyone was looking my way. I gave them a brief nod, and they all looked away. Now Isabel was shuffling from one foot to the other, telling me she was as anxious as I was. Finally the lift reached the lower ground level to the car park. As Isabel stepped out, I pulled her into a darkened corner before anyone saw us and pushed against the wall. Dropping my laptop bag and grabbing her leg, I kissed her lips, grinding myself against her so she could see how desperate and hard I was for her.

"Do you see, Isabel? Do you see what you do to me? I need to take you right here, right now," I said between hard, needing kisses.

"*No.*"

She had a small smile on her lips. It didn't register straight away what she had said, but when my brain took her answer in, I rested my forehead on hers but not letting her go, not even an inch.

"What do you mean *no*? I can't fucking wait any longer," I said, grinding myself against her again.

"Can you feel it? See what I mean? You're making me crazy with need."

"Did you forget what we agreed? This is still our workplace. Please, not here." She put both palms on my chest and pulled gently. I slowly let her leg go and clenched both my hands into fists, resting them behind her, trying to calm my breath and clear my head. Isabel didn't move away or touch me. She allowed me just to stay there, close to her but not touching her.

"Come on, let's get out of here. I need to get Lara. Why don't you go home, change, and then come over for dinner with us?" she said, almost whispering. I couldn't talk yet. I was so bloody worked up and had so much pent-up frustration that everything combined made my bloody pure steel, so I just nodded, grabbed my bag, and gave her a peck on the cheek, then went straight to my car without looking again on her direction. If I did, I wouldn't be able to leave.

On the way home, I contemplated my feelings. How could she make me feel so out of control, so desperate for her, so crazy with need? It was worse than when I was just a teenager, which, by the way, was when my dick had a life of its own. Isabel seemed to command all of me, and I can't for the life of me understand why or how. Jessica always made me crazy and, our sex life was a good one—or so I thought before she cheated on me—but now, with Isabel, it's like I need her so bad that no amount of hand jobs could satisfy me, only her. I've known her for only a month or so, and already I can't imagine a day without her. It scares me like hell.

CHAPTER 13

Isabel

As Jack headed to his car, I had to lean against the wall and let out a breath to steady myself. God help me, I don't know where I got the strength to say no to him. He is so hot when he loses control. God, we almost had sex in the company's car park. We need to be more careful. If someone had seen us, our lives would have gotten much more complicated.

Lara was feeling a little under the weather when I picked her up from school. I put my hand on her forehead.

"Oh, sweet pea, you're coming down with something. You are slightly hot." "I have a sore throat, Mummy."

"Okay, when we get home, you take some CALPOL and lie down until dinner is ready." "Okay."

"Right, I need to tell you something, sweet pea. I know it's not a great day, and if you don't feel up to it, I'll cancel it."

"What is it, Mummy?"

"Jack is coming for dinner tonight. Is that okay, baby?"

"Jack?" she almost shouted with renewed energy, her eyes shining and a smile brightening her face.

"Come down. So I take it is okay with you?" I said, smiling at her.

"Of course it's okay, Mummy. Wait, is that a date, Mummy? Do you want me to go to Grandma's?"

"No, it's not a date." I looked at her seriously, pursing my lips, thinking about how I should tell her Jack was now my boyfriend.

"Jack and I ... Jack and I are now ..."

I couldn't say it. I looked at her sideways, and I could see her smile growing.

"Mummy, is Jack your boyfriend?" she said, half-turning to me on her seat. "Yes," I whispered, looking forward to the road ahead.

"*Yeah, yes, yes.* Finally! Grandma did tell me it wouldn't take long." "What? What did Grandma say?" I said, shocked at her statement.

"She just said that you were in love with Jack and if he knew what was best for him, he would ask you to be his girlfriend before that other bloke, William, snatched you."

"She did not say that." "Yes, she did," she said.

"God, now I know what you talk about when you with her. Is my love life that interesting?"

"Well, yeah. Even Aunty Lizzy said you were head over heels for Jack, as he was over you."

"Oh God, my 8-year-old is telling me she has serious adult conversations about my love life. What is it going to be next? Are you going to tell me whom I should marry?" I said, feeling so embarrassed. Lara just laughed and shook her head.

"You're funny, Mummy. If Jack is your boyfriend, surely you will marry him." At that, I laughed out loud.

"Oh, baby, what am I going to do with you?" She was smirking and lifted her little head, as if she felt proud of her answer.

When we were home, I went for aquick shower and put on a maxi-dress—comfortable yet nottotallycasual, ideal for a home-cooked dinner with the man I love.

Wait, what did I just think? No, no, no, not love ... like, yeah, the man I like.

I was so distracted by my thoughts as I was cooking that I didn't hear the doorbell ring.

Lara, however, jumped from the kitchen table chair and ran to the door to open it.

"He's here, he's here," she was shouting on her way to the door. I just shook my head, smiling and thinking how Jack had a way of warming people's hearts. It amazed me. I heard Lara giggling, and when I turned from the stove, there he was, in fitted jeans, a dark red shirt with three opened buttons and sleeves rolled to his elbows, hair spiked. Jack was like a bloody sex god with the cheeky smirk I so love and his green gorgeous eyes that get me every time I catch their gaze.

"Hiya," was all I could muster. I turned away so his deep gaze wouldn't distract me any further. "Dinner won't take long."

He chuckled, and Lara, of course, started to jump up and down.

"Jack, do you want to see the song I wrote? I just finished it, and I think you're going to love it."

"Of course," he said with enthusiasm.

"Oh wait, Lara. Could you perhaps play it after dinner?" I said nervously without looking their way.

"Oh, Mummy I just can't wait to show Jack. Can I at least show him the lyrics?" For whatever reason, Jack was quiet, and my hands were shaking. I always get nervous for the tiniest thing, but this was ridiculous. We were supposed to be boyfriend and girlfriend, and I was acting like a teenage virgin.

Come on, Isabel, get over it. You already did the deed with him. Well, more than the deed. You did ... stop it, stop it. This isn't helping.

The next thing I realized, Jack was close behind me. "Isabel, you okay?" he whispered, making me jump. "Oh, yes,"

"Sorry, I didn't want to frighten you," he said, taking a small step back.

"You all right, Mummy? You look ill." Lara said, coming to me with concern in her eyes. I smiled at her and put a hand on my forehead. I felt clammy with nerves, but otherwise, I was okay.

"I'm okay, sweet pea. You, on the other hand, are not. So you need to take it easy. You are still flushed, so no running around or jumping around either. Go on, show Jack the lyrics and then we'll have dinner." I looked to Jack and gave him a small smile and a slight nod. He was concerned, I could see it.

What is wrong with me? This is what I wanted, him here interacting with Lara as he is, having dinner with us. God, this was more difficult than I expected. What if this doesn't work? What if I only bring trouble to his divorce case. This is too soon. What if he realizes that me having a child already is not what he wants and, when it all ends, both Lara and I get hurt? Lara loves him—I can see that—and it would kill me if this doesn't work out and Lara suffers.

I rested my head on the kitchen cabinet and sighed. "Please, God, help me," I whispered.

I finished dinner. Today, I cooked a Portuguese dish, *frango bebado*, accompanied by rice and a traditional Portuguese salad. Since I was a child I had always loved this dish. My mum used to cooked it when we had guests. It's chicken cooked in a red wine sauce.

"Dinner is ready," I shouted from the kitchen. "It smells divine," Jack said, smiling at me.

"Well, this is one of my favourite dishes. I just hope you like it." "I'm sure I will."

"It's nice, but I prefer *prego no prato*," Lara said. I laughed at Jack's expression. He was looking at Lara as if he hadn't understood a word she said. She looked at him and rolled her eyes.

"Jack, you really should learn Portuguese now that you are my Mummy's boyfriend." I choked on my own saliva. Jack just smiled and looked at me with a lifted eyebrow. "Maybe I should, seeing that I am now your Mummy's boyfriend—you're right." I felt my face go up in flames. I changed the subject back to food.

"*Prego no prato* is just steak, egg, rice, and salad—that's all," I said, opening a bottle of wine. Jack was still smirking and looking straight at me. I only spared a few glances between my lashes.

"Sorry, I didn't ask. Do you prefer red or white?" I asked, stopping myself from opening the red wine bottle.

"But you don't drink," Jack queried.

"Well, I don't, but you do, and I have been told that this is a red wine dinner, but I don't know if you like red wine."

"Red wine is perfect, thank you," he said.

"Okay, so this is from back home. My uncle has a vineyard. It's small, but it produces excellent wine—so I am told by everyone in the family." I smiled. Jack did that silly thing where he swirled the wine in the glass, smelling it, and then taking a small sip. He closed his eyes.

"Mmm, well, this is excellent all right. This should be served at the best restaurants in England. It would have great success."

"Well, my uncle doesn't like to export. He has the old-fashion mindset. What is national is the best and should be appreciated nationally, not internationally. Yeah, I know. He is lovely—don't get me wrong—but he can be a little intense with foreigners."

"Are you trying to intimidate me so I won't want to go to Portugal and meet him?" he said, smiling a little.

"No, I am simply stating a fact. He was really unhappy when I got married with Sam because he wasn't Portuguese. He didn't even come to our wedding because of it," I said, realizing too late that I had mentioned Sam while Lara was at the table. I looked at her, and she was staring at me.

"Oh, sweet pea, I'm sorry. I didn't mean to ..." I looked from her to Jack, and he was fiddling with his napkin, trying to look busy.

"Mummy, it's okay." She looked at Jack. "It's great that Mummy talks about my daddy with you. He would have liked you," she said. We were both shocked at her statement. It was so quiet; the only sounds were the cutlery on the plates while we ate. Jack broke the silence.

"This is so tasty, Isabel. I haven't had a home-cooked dinner for a while, and this is probably the best I've had."

"Thank you, but I'm sure your chef cooks spectacular food."

"What chef? I don't have a chef. Okay, when I was married, yes, we had a chef, and when I lived with my parents, but believe me, I've never had food like this—comfort food, without that fancy sauces and garnishes. Believe me, it can get tedious. You know what I used to do? I used to sneak into Ian's house sometimes at dinner time so I could eat proper food. My mum always knew I didn't like fancy food, but she couldn't cook, so there was no other way."

"Well, you will get fat with my mummy cooking. She cooks really nice food. All my friends say so when they come over," Lara said to Jack.

"Is that so? So you think I'll get a fat belly?" Lara nodded seriously, and I just smiled. "That won't do. She won't want me then," he said with a frightened expression. I loved the way he joked with Lara.

"Oh, you don't have to worry about that. She won't leave you. She loves you, silly." I dropped my fork loudly into my plate, and my face for the second time today felt like a volcano—so damn hot.

"Oh, *does she* now? She loves me, does she? That's good to know," he said playfully, looking at me. I just gave him a little smile, but I was sure it looked more like agrimace.

When dinner was over, Jack was a gentleman helping me tidy the kitchen. It was funny, actually. He kept asking, "Where does this go?" in a way that was so damn sexy. Watching him go around the kitchen putting things away was starting to get me all hot andbothered.

"Mummy, can we go to the living room so I can play the song now?"

"Sure, we all finished here anyway." Jack grabbed my hand and planted a little kiss on it while Lara was skipping in front. We sat on the sofa while Lara played and sang. She was as amazing as ever. At the end, we clapped, but she had a slight worried expression. Jack asked what was wrong, and she started to talk about the lyrics, whether they fit with the melody she had written. They were going over it, and Jack sat at the piano and started to play it, making a few changes. I was completely shocked. I didn't know he played, let alone wrote, music. I looked at both of them sitting there talking technicalities, and in that moment, I saw us as a family, a real family. Jack was so great with Lara—patient, sweet, and loving. It all made me so happy that he was in our lives.

"Mummy, can we watch a movie in the cinema room?" "Aren't you tired?" I asked, concerned.

"No, I feel better actually," she said.

"I called Aunty Lizzy and Mark to come over for drinks. They should be here soon. Do you think you can wait for them?" Jack looked at me surprised. I had forgotten to mention it to him. *Shit.*

"Oh, sorry. I completely forgot to mention this. Is that okay with you?"

He smiled kindly. "Of course it is. I really enjoy their company, Isabel. It'll be great." Not long after, Lizzy and Mark arrived. Lara jumped straight to Lizzy, who lifted her up and squeezed her hard.

"A-aunty Lizzy, I can't breathe," Lara said playfully. "How are you, my little nugget?"

"I'm great. Jack is here too. You were right. He is my mummy's boyfriend now." Oh God, I couldn't get more embarrassed if wanted to.

"Of course he is. He would be silly not to," she said, looking at him with a smirk.

"So true," he said, smiling wide. He grabbed me closer to him. I let him, but my face was on fire.

"You okay, Izzy? You look like you are about to explode," Lizzy said, smiling cheekily. "I'm fine, Lizzy," I said, giving her a menacing look. I turned to go down to the cinema room. I heard giggling all the way down. Lizzy is the cheekiest person I know. She is always looking for something to tease me about, and she now has something to work with. God help me.

At the end of the movie, Lara was asleep. Jack offered to take her into bed, and I accepted. We both went upstairs, and I made sure Lara was fast asleep in her little princess bed. Once I closed Lara's bedroom door, very carefully so that she wouldn't wake up, Jack grabbed me and kissed me with hunger, squeezing my butt, grinding against me. It was so hot that I almost dragged him straight to my bedroom, but I remembered Lizzy and Mark were still downstairs, so with tremendous effort, I reminded Jack of this fact.

"Lizzy ... Mark," he grunted. "Can't we just say we are tired?" he said half-jokingly. Yes, only half-jokingly; I could hear the hopefulness in his voice.

"No, I don't feel tired, and I don't lie," I said, smiling. I planted a small, soft kiss on his lush lips. His eyes were again so damn dark with need that my sex clenched.

"But I promise you that when they leave, I will have my way with you, and this time, it will be you who ends up strapped to the bed," I said, leaving him behind without saying anything further.

"I thought you weren't coming back," Lizzy said. "Stop," said Mark, smiling.

"Why, baby? Look at them. They've obviously been making out. Maybe it's time for us to leave," she said, chuckling, making Mark chuckle too.

"You know, Lizzy, I remember a few occasions when you and Mark here did more than just make out while I was visiting, don't you?" I said, smiling. It was a challenge to both of them. They widened their eyes, and Mark was so red with embarrassment that it made Jack laugh hard.

"Good foryou, man," Jack said, high-fiving Mark.

"Well, it's not my fault. Mark was hot as hell, and let me tell you the sex ..."

"Ah, stop right there. Shit, I don't want to hear about that," I said, covering my ears. "That backfired so fast I didn't see it coming," said Jack, still laughing, but this time it was at me.

"Whatever," I mumbled.

"Okay, now seriously. I'm really happy for you, sweetheart. You deserve to be happy again, and Jack is a stand-up guy, aren't you, Jack?" She turned quickly to him, giving him her mean look.

"I am Mrs Elizabeth Bennett." At her full name, she came closer to him.

"That's the last time you say my full name, you understand? My name is Lizzy," she said seriously. Jack took a little step back with both hands raised.

"Of course. Sorry, I never thought I couldn't use your full name. My apologies." Lizzy looked at both Mark and me, and we knew she was messing with Jack. We couldn't hold it in any longer. We all burst out laughing, apart from Jack, who was frowning.

"What?" he kept asking. Bless him, Lizzy was going to have so much fun with him that I felt sorry for the lad.

"Oh, baby, she's messing with you." He let out a sigh.

"Great," he said, grabbing me and planting a kiss on my lips. That definitely shut me up. "Oh, okay, that's enough. You can do more of that smooching when we've gone."

Jack chuckled. I was already too hot, and I didn't know if I could actually hold for that long.

We spent a few more hours drinking. Yes, I actually drank one cocktail, which Jack prepared, and I can say I was feeling tipsy as hell.

"It's so hot in here, isn't it?" I said, feeling as if I were in a desert. I started to lift my maxi-dress's hem, and Jack quickly stopped me.

"Hold on, baby. Not here," he said. This brought a laugh from Lizzy.

"I think that's our cue to leave. The girl is in heat," she said, or I think that's what she said.

"Oh no, don't go. I'm not tired, and it's still too early anyway," I said, or rather slurred.

"Jack and I have lots of time to have sex, don't worry. Oh God, now that I think of it, I am so fucking desperate to fuck you baby," I said to Jack.

"Okay, it's definitely time to go," Mark said. Jack was holding me, and I started to kiss his neck.

"God, you smell good. Hmmm."

"Isabel, let's just see our guest to the door first, okay, baby?" he whispered. "But I need you," I said, completely forgetting Lizzy and Mark were there. "No need, Jack. We know our way out," Lizzy said, smiling.

"It's okay. Isabel is okay, right?" he said, looking into my eyes. I just nodded and followed them, or tried to, as Jack kept pulling me up the stairs. The damn stairs kept moving in weird ways under my feet.

"Well, now you know why she doesn't drink," Lizzy whispered to Jack.

"I heard that. I don't drink because it's disgusting, but Jack is so talented, even at making cocktails. God, Jack, what are you rubbish at?" I managed to say. Jack just laughed, shaking his head.

"Okay, will you be all right?" Lizzy asked Jack. "Sure, don't worry."

"If you need anything, let me know. If you're not sure about something relating to Lara, give me a buzz, okay?"

"Don't worry. We'll be okay, I promise." "Well, have fun." Lizzy winked at me. "Oh, I will," I slurred.

When Jack closed the front door, I pushed him hard against the door and kissed him passionately, fiddling with his shirt buttons.

"Off, off," I said, desperate to feel his firm chest. He didn't hesitate, taking off his shirt as quickly as possible. I opened his belt, popped his jeans' button, and zipped down. As fast but as gently as I could, I took his already very, very erect dick. Jack growled when I had him in my fist.

"Fuck, you are so fucking sexy," he said between kisses. I lowered myself and took him in my mouth. At the first feeling of my mouth, he growled even louder.

"Fuck. Isabel, Lara." He was struggling to speak while I worked him. I stopped for a second.

"You better stop that growling, Mr Wolf."

"Shit, even when you insult me, you're so sexy." He put both hands on my head and started to thrust slowly into my mouth, moaning. I could tell when he was close because the thrusts became more erratic and his breathing was now short, quick pants. I stopped and stood up, kissing him again on the mouth. This act alone made my knickers even wetter. I grabbed my maxi-dress and took it off.

"It's too hot to be wearing clothes, don't you think?" I said, looking at him there with his trousers at his knees and his erection bobbing like crazy.

"Isabel," he said, stepping closer to me. I stepped back again, playing with him.

"You won't be able to catch me with your trousers down, lad," I said, taunting him while moving backwards, towards the kitchen.

"Oh, I can catch you if I want to, pants at my knees or not. Nothing can keep you from me, Isabel. Not now, not ever," he said, looking into my eyes and moving forward with careful steps, one hand holding his pants, stalking me like a wild animal stalking its prey.

"So, what are you waiting for?" I said. Then I tumbled. When I thought I would hit the floor, Jack caught me in his arms.

"I told you I wouldn't let you go." He lifted me up so fast my head spun. I didn't know how, but the next thing I knew, I was sitting on the kitchen island. Jack was sucking and licking my nipples. I could hear only my moans. He made me so hot.

"Now, Jack, now," I said with so much need in my voice.

"I thought you said I would be the one strapped to the bed," he said, smiling as he kissed my neck.

"The night is young. Now fuck me before I rape you," I said, or slurred—I'm not sure. My brain was not working properly. All I know is that I needed Jack to take me hard. Jack lifted me up and brought me down into his thick shaft in one quick thrust. We both moaned.

"Hard baby, hard," I said breathlessly. Jack complied, working in fast, hard thrusts. It didn't take long before I was exploding around him. I was being a bit too loud, so Jack covered my mouth.

"Shhhh, keep it down, baby. We don't want to wake up Lara," he said, panting while still thrusting. When my spasms ceased, Jack came out of me and turned me around. He extended both my arms on the kitchen island so my breasts were resting on the marble. He grabbed my ass and slapped it.

"Shit."

"Oh, baby. I need to take your ass one of these days. I need all of you. Mine." He sounded so possessive and hot. I know, I was sick. How could I like a possessive man? I just couldn't get my head around it. Jack slammed into me again, grabbing my hips and thrusting really fast. It hit straight on my G point, and I was soon too close.

"Jack, ah ... oh God." He kept going.

"Come for me baby, come."

Just as he asked, my body gave in, and I came again with such intensity that I felt myself lifting off the kitchen island. I was groaning so much. Jack wasn't far behind. I was still spasming hard when he came. We just stayed there for a while until our breathing slowed down. I felt all the juices coming out and starting to drip down my leg. I reached for paper towels and cleaned myself while Jack leaned over island, resting his forehead on the cool marble top.

"I love you," he said. I could see he was afraid, maybe of my reaction, but I knew he did love me, as I knew very well that I loved him. But I wasn't ready to say it, not yet, so I just kissed him instead. He smiled, and we lay there and embraced, both of us feeling so calm and happy. For so long I hadn't felt this happy. Yes, I had been happy with Lara, but this was different. I was now complete again, and it brought tears to my eyes, knowing that I felt this all again, feelings I thought I'd never have again.

After that night, we decided we would see each other every day after work, have dinner at my place, tuck Lara in together, have our sex session, and then off he would go. Okay, most nights he stayed over and left early in the morning for a fresh change before work, but we wanted to keep it like this until his divorce was finalized. Jack was confident that would be soon.

We have been in a relationship for three months now, and today was the last day Jessica had to sign the papers before Jack's solicitors go for plan C. Don't ask me what that plan is, because I don't want to know, but I'm praying that she will just sign those damn papers.

CHAPTER 14

Jack

Today I was feeling so anxious that I hardly ate anything. Isabel and I were in a great place, but I wanted to take it further and ask her to move in together. We could buy something new, something together, to be ours. She has been great both at work and at home. She is such a good mum and an amazing girlfriend, always making sure I had time for my family and friends, not that I have a lot of friends. Ian is the only person I can truly call a friend, and we still go for drinks a few times a week, but we are spending less time together because I feel I need to spend every minute I have with Isabel. She always says it's good for me to spend time with the people I love. That makes me laugh, because she knows I love her. I said it so many times before, but I have yet to hear her say it. I know she loves me, but she isn't ready—maybe because of this divorce. I need it to be over so we can move on with our lives. I want to take Isabel and Lara on holidays, on outings as a family, not as my PA. I want to give her gifts, everything she deserves, but until the divorce is settled, my solicitors have advised me not to.

"Okay, so you are happy with everything we've been discussing?" Anthony, one of my solicitors, asked me.

"Yes, everything is exactly how I want it. We need this to be signed today, guys. I don't want to leave without Jessica signing the bloody papers, understood?" I said to all three team members.

"Mrs Corner, I want to thank you for working together with Anthony and John on this.

You have been great through all this."

"No problem, Jack. I just want to make sure you get what you want in the fastest way possible, and I'm glad to help."

Mrs Corner is what you call posh, from the way she speaks to the way she presents herself. I am very glad I have her in my corner. Everyone who deals with her adores her and respects her.

"Okay, so we have fifteen minutes before the meeting starts. Let's have a ten-minute break."

I stood and went to the rooftop garden at the mediation centre. There were a few people there smoking. I guessed they were there for the same reason as I was, because their grim expressions were close to mine. I called Isabel. I needed to hear her voice. It was hard not being able to bring her with me. She did offer, but we both knew I couldn't accept.

"Hello," Isabel answered. "Hiya, it's just me."

"Yeah, I know. I can read the name on the screen," she said with a smile on her voice.

Just hearing her made a big grin spread on my lips.

"Oh, so you saved my number as 'Gorgeous Boyfriend'?" I teased her.

"No, that was too long. I just saved you as 'BOSS'." Oh she was good at this. "Good thing then, as I am the *boss* in all respects." That made her chuckle.

"You wish. I can remind you later if you like who really is the boss in—oh, I don't know— something that makes you go like ..." Then she made a deep growling sound, trying to imitate me. To be honest, she got it pretty close.

"All right, all right, you can show me later. I won't complain," I said, smiling like a teenage boy. The few people there were now looking at me, so I turned my back to them. "I just wanted to hear your voice and tell you I love you before I head for the last battle— or at least I hope it will be."

"Yeah, well maybe it won't even be a battle at all. Maybe she will just sign the papers and that will be it. Don't stress, okay? Everything will be okay, and I will be waiting for you whatever the outcome." It is because of this and more that I love this woman. She always has the right thing to say at the right moment.

"Thank you, baby. I can't wait to see you. All right, it's time to get this show on the road.

Bye, baby."

"Bye, Jack, and good luck."

When I entered the room with my legal team, Jessica was taken by surprise. She did not expect to see me with three solicitors around me.

"Well, well, well, I see you're doing well at Reeds to be able to pay so many solicitors." "Ms Jackson, thank you for coming today." Anthony welcomed Jessica with her maiden name, and I smirked at her.

"*Mrs Reed*. I am Mrs Reed still, so I would appreciate it if you treated me as such."

"Oh yes, my apologies," Anthony said, smiling, letting her know he wasn't really sorry at all. *Oh, this will be fun.*

"Welcome, everyone. I believe Mr Reed's legal team has drawn a new contract as per our lastdiscussion?"

"Yes, we have. Can I say that this will be our last attempt to come to an agreement? If Mrs Reed does not sign this, we will file the divorce on the grounds of infidelity. As you know, we have a file with witnesses and other things to prove her affair," Mrs Corner said, getting straight to thepoint.

"Okay, okay, we are here to come to an agreement. We want to avoid the courts. Isn't that right, Mrs Reed?" the mediator said, smiling kindly to Jessica.

"Well, my solicitor and I have had a long discussion, and I think I'll chance it in court." "*What?*" I shouted, not believing this bitch was actually stupid enough to go to court. "What, Jack, you scared I'll get shares in the company?" she said with an evil grin. "No, I'm not scared at all. I just thought you weren't so stupid enough to think you will get more if you go to court."

"Okay, come down, everyone. Mrs Reed, can I ask what made you come to that decision?"

"Well, a few things, actually, but the fact that Mr Reed is sleeping with his PA is the main one."

"Hold on a second. Are you saying the reason you didn't sign the papers is that I ... I'm sleeping with my PA? Unbelievable. You cheated on me, Jessica. You fucked my best friend's brother, and now you're not signing because I am sleeping with my PA? Are you joking with me?"

"Mr Reed, calmed down please," the mediator intervened. I could not believe what I was hearing.

"Mrs Reed, aren't you both living in separate places, living separate lives?" the mediator asked.

"Yes, so?" Jessica answered as if it were the most natural thing.

"What I am hearing is that you both living different lives, and so the divorce is the only logical thing to do. I understand you might not be happy about Mr Reed's choices, but you both chose to get divorce, am I right?"

"Yes, but I don't want to get divorced anymore. I raised this with Jack already." "Yes, and I told you that you were crazy to think I would go back after what you've done."

"Look, Mrs Reed, Mr Reed's legal team put together the new contract, and you have had a chance to go over it with your solicitor. I understand you want to go to court, but this will get really messy, and it can take two or more years to be decided. In the meantime, you would both be stuck in your lives, unable to move forward. Have you really thought this through?" the mediator insisted.

"Jack, let's try again, honey. I love you, and I really can't live apart anymore," Jessica aid.

"Jessica, sign the damn papers and get this divorced filed. I will not take you back, not in a million years. Sign them and move on. I have been more than generous already. If we go to court, you probably will probably get even less, and you will have to pay for legal fees too."

"I can't," she said.

"Okay, look, let's take a fifteen-minute break and let Mrs Reed gather her thoughts with her solicitor. Is that okay?" the mediator asked all of us. We all nodded, and I left the room, furious that Jessica was still playing games. I hated her, now more than ever. She was the only thing standing in the way of my happiness. How could Isabel wait for my divorce to come through if Jessica don't sign the papers? It could take years for this to be over. I sat in the reception area with my elbows on my knees and my hands on my head.

"It'll be over soon. We have a plan. Jack, trust us. It won't take long for her to change her mind," Anthony said.

"Oh yeah? Do you think she gives a shit? She will go to court because she thinks she will be entitled much more as the years progress and my money continues to grow."

"No, she won't. She is not going to want to go to court. I have something new. You haven't seen yet," he said, crouching low and whispering. "I just need to go back to the meeting room right now and hand this to her solicitor." He showed me the file.

"What's that?"

"It's pictures of Jessica and two different judges having sex. Yes, I know. I got an investigator to follow her. We just need to let her know that whatever the judges have agreed to won't hold up because we have proof that she's messed around with them to gain their favour."

"Well, she can say they haven't agreed to anything."

"Maybe, if we only had the pictures, but we have recordings too. You will be surprised to hear their conversations. Now just give me five minutes alone with them, okay?" he said, smiling at me. I was shocked. This man is really clever. Thank God I listened to my dad.

"Go," I whispered, a glimmer of hope in my voice.

About ten minutes later, Anthony came back smiling with his hands in his pockets. "Well?" I asked.

"I think they are ready to carry on with the meeting. Let's go." I jumped to my feet.

Jessica was so red, she was furious, and if looks could kill, I would be dead right now. "Welcome back, everyone. So, Mrs Reed, have you had a chance to go over what we discussed and come to a conclusion?" the mediator asked.

"Yes, Mrs Reed and I had a chat, and she is ready to sign the papers now—with one condition. Mrs Reed asks Mr Reed to go for a final dinner with her, a farewell of sorts."

"What? No," I said. How could I sit at the same table and have a meal with this woman, who has brought me only misery?

"May I just say, it's the only way Mrs Reed will sign today, now," her solicitor said, looking straight at me.

"Take it, Jack. I know is not ideal, but just endure this one dinner, and you will be completely free of her," Anthony whispered in my ear. I looked at all the members of my legal team, and they nodded in agreement.

"Fine, one last dinner, and that is it, Jessica. Now sign the damn papers." She smirked. I was sure she had something up her sleeve, but I had no idea what it was. She signed the papers with a little scowl but didn't look at me. Anthony slapped my back lightly, and I shook hands with Jessica's solicitor.

"Congratulations, both of you, for coming to an amicable agreement. Good luck to you both," the mediator said, shaking my hand and Jessica's in turn. I was so relieved, I wanted to talk to Isabel to tell her the good news. I ran outside and dialled her number. It went straight to voicemail. I tried again and again, but it went to voicemail again.

"You can pick me up tonight at 8 p.m. You know where to pick me up from, so I expect you to be on time, darling," Jessica said, coming from behind me.

"Tonight?"

"Yes, tonight at 8 p.m."

"Not tonight. Some other day," I said, trying to dismiss this. I needed time to prepare myself to share a meal with this bitch, whom I hated so much now.

"Nope, I want to go to dinner tonight. You agreed to one final dinner." "Yes, but I didn't say when," I said, trying to get her off me.

"I can always go back up there and cancel the whole thing."

Shit, she really is a bitch.

"Fine, at 8 p.m."

"Great. And Jack, I want to go to Le Dame de Pic. You know I like their food." I just turned and got into my car. I tried Isabel again, and this time it rang. She picked up on the third ring.

"Hello."

"Hi, baby." Just hearing her say hello made me smile. "Hi, is the meeting finished?"

"Yep."

"Aaaand?"

"And I'm on my way to yours right now."

"Okay. Come on, Jack. I'm dying here. What happened?" I remained quiet for a little while. "Oh, God, Jack, she didn't sign again. I'm sorry, sweetheart."

"Oh, she signed them."

"Wait what? She signed them?" I heard her squeaking in delight.

"Oh, Jack, I'm so pleased. Thank God you won't have to deal with her again."

Oh shit, I need to tell her.

"Well ..." I didn't know how I should tell her this. "Well what?" she asked.

"Baby, I need to tell you something."

Fuck, how am I going to tell my girlfriend that I have dinner with my now ex-wife today?

"Need to tell me what?" she said. I could hear the worry in her voice. "She agreed to sign the papers today with one condition."

"Okay, what is the condition?"

"I need to have a final dinner with her ... today ... at eight."

Isabel was quiet, and I started to worry that she would dump me. "Okay."

"Okay?"

"Yeah, okay. I guess it could be worse, right? She could ask for a farewell kiss, or ..."

Okay, she sounded a little jealous. I couldn't see her face, but her voice was a bit bitter. I had never heard her like that.

"Hey, hey, baby, don't be upset. You know I don't love her anymore. I actually hate her. But the point is I agreed to it just so she would sign the damn papers, which she did. Isabel, you don't need to be worried. You know that, right?"

She was quiet for a little longer than I wanted. "Yeah, I know. It's just ..."

"Yeah, I know. Look, I'll be over in about twenty minutes. We can talk over a nice cold drink in the courtyard. What do you say?"

"Sure. See you in a bit. Bye." "Bye."

After speaking to Isabel, I called my dad and Ian to let them know the news. They were both really happy for me, but then I mentioned the dinner, and they both said the same thing.

"Be careful. This might be another of her games. Don't drink alcohol, and made sure you don't leave your drink alone."

After speaking to Ian and asking him to be there as well, at a table farther away, Ian agreed that this was a great idea. He would keep an eye out for me. That made me feel so much better about this dinner. When I got to Isabel's place, I felt nervous. I knew she wasn't over the moon about this dinner, but I had to tell her. She needed to know even if it hurt, which I know it did; I could hear it in hervoice.

"Hey!" I kissed her pink lips before she could say anything else. "Hmmm, that's the best congratulatory kiss I've ever had."

"Oh yeah? Wait until later then. I might just top it off," she said, smiling against my lips, kissing me a few more sweet wet kisses.

"Come on. I have cold freshly-squeezed lemonade in the courtyard at the back," she said, grabbing my hand and pulling me with her.

"Where's Lara?"

"She's at Sara's house. Sara is one of her friends from music lessons."

"Oh yes, she mentioned her a few times."

"So, dinner, huh?" she said, taking a long sip from her lemonade glass, trying to hide her face.

"Yep. I spoke to Ian about it, and we came up with a plan. I'm picking her up at eight tonight. We are going to this high-end joint in the Four Seasons Hotel, but what she doesn't know is that Ian will be there too, a few tables away from us. Ian actually made the reservations himself so he could organize the seating. This way, he can keep an eye out for me."

Isabel sighed loudly, looking at her hands.

"I just ... I feel uncomfortable with this. I know how you feel, but what I understand from you and your family and friend is that Jessica likes to play games. I'm afraid this is one of them."

"Well, that is the reason Ian will be there—to make sure any game she has going on won't work. Please, Isabel, I can't do this without you. I need you to trust me and just believe that everything will be okay."

"Okay. I do trust you. It is hard to know my gorgeous boyfriend is having dinner with his hot-as-hell ex-wife, but I do trust you." I pulled her into my lap and kissed her passionately.

"I love you, Isabel de Sousa."

I was ready. After calling Isabel to make sure she was okay, I called Ian to check if everything was in place. When I arrived at Jessica's, she hugged me and tried to kiss me, but I was too quick, turning my face. She planted her lips on my cheek. I pulled away from her quickly and got her into my Jaguar F-PACE.

"Couldn't you get a limo?" she said, irritated.

"What for? I thought I was taking you to a final dinner, not the Oscars," I threw back at her.

"Oh, darling, you see, we sound so normal, so married."

"Well, we are not married anymore. You signed the paper today, remember?" "Humph, yeah. So, tell me, how is dear old Dad?"

"*My* dear old dad is fine. In fact, he is wonderful since you signed the papers," I said, trying to get at her.

"Good, then I should pay him a visit one of these days. I bet he would like to ... have dinner," she said, smirking, goading me.

"You can only try, but I know my dad. He will most likely throw you out, so I would think twice before showing up."

She chuckled. "Oh, Jack, are you jealous?"

"Why would I be jealous of you? I simply know how my father feels about you, so I thought I should warn you before you went and embarrassed yourself. But by all means, go ahead and show up at his doorstep," I said with a little shrug.

When we arrived, I didn't open the door for Jessica; I simply gave the keys to the valet and went straight in. Jessica was behind me, mumbling.

"Reservation for two under Reed please," I said to the young girl in the restaurant. "Oh, yes. Please follow me."

She sat us in a little booth. It was far too romantic, but at least Jessica was on the opposite side. I picked my menu and hid behind it.

"Jack are you going to mope all evening? This is supposed to be fun, darling."

I couldn't believe she actually thought I could have fun with her. She was a fucking lunatic.

"Are fucking joking? Do you really think I would enjoy spending time with you? Jessica, I detest you. You only caused me pain, and by continuously refusing to sign the papers and playing your games, you made me hate you more than anything in this world. If you think I really want to be here, you're stupider than I thought." I kept my voice low but mean. I wanted her to get it through her head that there wouldn't be a minute of happiness on this dinner. She sighed.

"Fine. I just wanted us to end this in a good note, not being like this. I did love you, and in my own way still do. Let's stop arguing and just have a nice meal; then you go and live happily ever after with that ..."

She didn't finish her sentence, maybe because of the look I gave her.

We kept quiet during our meal. A few times, I looked around to see if I could find Ian. I thought he was at the bar area, but the gentleman was wearing a grey hat and was facing the bar, so I couldn't be sure it was him. While Jessica made attempts at conversation, I kept my answers as short as possible, mostly "yes", "no", and "I don't know". She didn't care. She kept talking about how many things she had done and places she had been since we split. I couldn't have cared less. I just wanted to end this ridiculous evening. When the dinner was over, I got up, and we were outside when we were swamped with flashes of cameras and paparazzi firing question after question at us. I was shocked. Jessica was on my arm, tugging me close to her and smiling. When I realized what was happening, I pulled away from her.

"This was your plan? You stupid, stupid woman." I then turned to one of the photographers. "You want to know our situation? Here is the front-page news. We're finally divorced, and I couldn't be happier. This was our last dinner. Now, have a good night, everyone." I didn't even look back to Jessica. I went into my car and drove off with speed. I couldn't believe she tried to make a show out of me. What did she have to gain by the media thinking we were still married? It didn't make sense.

Soon after, Ian called me. "Yes?"

"Shit, Jack. You okay?" "Yes, I am now."

"This was a shit show. Jessica was telling them that you were still very much in love, but because of your statement, they all laughed it off, and she was the fool."

"Good. Maybe now she'll stop playing games. I've had enough of them."

"It's okay, mate. It's over—that is the most important thing. Are you going to Isabel's?" "Yep. Can't wait to see her, man."

"I bet," he said, laughing a little. "She is an exceptional woman."

"That, my friend, she is. Don't let her go."

"I don't intend to. Thank you for tonight, mate." "Anytime. Have a good night, okay."

"Bye." I ended the call.

Now I felt a little better knowing I was going to see Isabel and that the charade was over. Finally, I could ask Isabel to move in together, take her on holidays and weekends away. Oh, God, I couldn't wait for my life to start.

When I parked on Isabel's drive, I found myself almost running to her front door. I pressed on the doorbell, and when Isabel opened the door, I crashed my lips into hers and grabbed her to me. She responded with the same desperation to feel me there with her.

"You took too long," she said, a bit upset.

"I'm sorry, baby. I'm here now, and I'm never leaving you," I said against her lips, not able to dislodge myself from her.

"Good, because I have something to show you."

She dragged me upstairs to her room, and, oh God, she showed me. She showed me every bit I wanted and desperately needed from her.

In the morning, we had breakfast, and I asked my dad if it would be okay to take one day off with Isabel to celebrate the divorce. He was okay with it, but Isabel complained for about two hours, saying that the weekend was only two days away and we could celebrate then. I, of course, would not wait two days. Today was the day I would spoil her. While she dropped Lara at school, I made arrangements for the day. I booked us a spa day. I needed a good massage with my beautiful girlfriend next to me. At the spa, they have a great restaurant, so I asked them to organize a romantic setting for us, with lots of red roses and Champagne, both in our suite and at the restaurant table. I also called my favourite jewellers to send me pictures of diamond bracelets, simple ones and intricate ones, which they did straight away. I picked a simple row of diamonds and asked them to deliver it to the spa. Finally, I called a good friend of mine who owns a chic clothing shop and ordered an evening gown for Isabel, along with shoes, also to be delivered to the spa. Everything was well organized, and I was feeling so happy. After we left Isabel's house, I went by my place to grab a tuxedo and a few things.

On the way, Isabel finally asked, "Okay, I can't wait anymore. Where are we going? I didn't bring a lot of things, and I wasn't sure if we were staying the night, so I asked Lizzy to pick Lara up from school and keep her until I get her."

"Don't worry, baby. I'll speak to Lizzy in a while. I'm sure she won't mind having Lara overnight."

"*What?* No, Jack, I can't impose on Lizzy like that. She has a life and a job she needs to get to in the morning."

"Don't worry. If the issue is money, I'll pay."

"Jack, it's not about the money. If it were, I would pay. I have money. The issue is that I have responsibilities, and so do other people."

"Okay, look, when we arrive wherever I'm taking you, we'll call Lizzy and see if it will be okay. If there is an issue, then we'll cut it short and go home. How does that sound?"

I could see her head already weighing her options.

"Fine. Jack, we need to make one thing clear. I have a daughter who I need to be there for. You need to understand that this can't happen often." She was worried that I would push Lara aside. I couldn't let her think that. I loved Lara, and I would never push her aside, but today was different; today was for us, as a couple.

"Isabel, I understand that. Please don't get me wrong. I love Lara, but today is different. Today I wanted to celebrate us. I am officially divorced, and I need to celebrate with the woman I love. Is that wrong?" She sighed and shook her head.

"No, it's okay. I just get scared sometimes." "Scared? Of what?"

"I don't know. Scared that this is moving too fast, scared that Lara will feel left out." "Okay, look, this weekend we go somewhere fun for Lara. We'll ask her what she wants to do, and we'll spend the whole weekend doing what she likes. What do you think?"

"Yeah, I think that will be nice. Thank you." She whispered the last part. She was looking at me with such a grateful expression. I grabbed her hand and kissed it.

"All will be okay."

The day was spectacular. We went for a swim before dinner, and Isabel put on the beautiful silver gown and shoes left on the bed earlier. She looked as gorgeous as ever.

"I can't believe you did all this. When did you do this exactly?" she said with one hand on her hip, so mumsy it made me laugh.

"A gentleman never tells his secrets," I said playfully. She smiled and came over to straighten my bowtie.

"There, you look like Agent 007."

"Oh, you didn't know? My name is Reed, Jack Reed," I said, trying to sound serious but failing.

"Oh, come on. Let's eat. I'm famished," she said, holding onto my arm.

"Wait, before we go, I have something I want you to have," I said, getting the bracelet box from the bedside table. "Here." She opened it and gasped.

"Oh, Jack, I can't take this. It's too much," she said. Of course she would say that.

"Not at all. This is nothing. You deserve so much more," I said, grabbing the bracelet and putting it around her wrist. "There, now you are perfect." She smiled at that, and we left the room.

We spent most weekends with Lara doing things she loved and some weekends with Isabel's mum. She is a wonderful lady, very independent, very much like Isabel. Normally in the evenings, we would have Lizzy, Mark, and Ian over to Isabel's place to have drinks. We got in a routine, which was okay, but I wanted really to buy a place for us. Isabel thought it was too early to do that, and she seemed not to want to leave her home. I understood that this was where she was happy, and for now I would be okay with it. I was really surprised one day. We were in a relationship for just over five months when she asked me to move into her house. I accepted, of course, because I wanted to live with her, but I felt a bit uncomfortable. This wasn't our place. This was her place. Life was good. We were in a great place, Lara's career was taking off, and Isabel kept the office as well as the home in order. I had to spend more time at the company, as I had now fully taken the reins. This meant longer hours, but I made sure my weekends were free to spend with my girls. Isabel mentioned William Hamilton a few times. Apparently they kept in touch, and he was even over few times for drinks with us. I still didn't like him. Maybe it was jealousy, but I just did not like the guy. He texted Isabel one night about 10 p.m., and that got to me.

"He's now texting you this late?"

"Who?" she said. She looked at her mobile, which was on the bed, and read the text. "He's asking if we are still seeing each other," she said with a sorry look in her face. I looked away.

"He still pining after you, I see," I said, a bit bitter.

"Hey, Jack, you know there is nothing going on between us, right? We are just friends, and I never meet with him if you're not with me."

"Well, you can always cut all contact," I threw back at her more harshly than I intended. "I'm sorry. I didn't mean it like that," I said, rubbing my hands in my face.

"Maybe you're right. It's not fair to you. If he still has hopes of getting with me, I need to end our friendship." I couldn't believe she was actually going to do this.

"Isabel, I don't you to stop seeing any of your friends because I don't feel comfortable." "I do, actually, because if you're not comfortable, then neither am I. We are together, and I love you."

Wait, she said she loved me. She actually said the words, the words she had never said before.

She noticed my shocked expression and smiled. She got on her knees and straddled me, coming closer to my face.

"I love you, Jack. I always have and always will."

With that, I grabbed her and we kissed. Well, we more than kissed; we made love, slow love, like we were doing it for the first time, and in a way, maybe we were. I had said the words awhile ago, but Isabel had never said them back until now. I knew she loved me, but hearing her say them made my heart swell in a way it never had.

Lara and I got along so well. She was such a great little girl, so easygoing, and it was impossible not to love her. Being in relationship with my PA was actually great. My schedule couldn't have been put together any better. She knew where to fit everything in the right place; even Lara's performances were there, and I didn't miss any of them. It made me feel so proud, as if I had accomplished something important every time I attended her performances. Other parents were starting to get to know me well at her school too. I would occasionally pick Lara up from school and drop her at home, then go back to work. Isabel always thought I was crazy, but I felt more close to both of them when I did little things like that. Work was always extremely busy, but because I had such a fantastic PA, I always had plenty help from her, and now I had added another PA to the team, an intern, Isabel was training, and things were going smoothly.

One day, I finished work early, as a client had to cancel a meeting. On my way home, I stopped at Tiffany's, and something overtook me. I asked them to design an engagement ring. Yes, I know, maybe it was a little early, but I was ready for the next step. I wasn't sure if Isabel was ready, so I started hinting about getting married to see her reaction. I needed to be sure she would be ready before I proposed. I didn't want to hear a no. I couldn't take the rejection. I explained to the design team what I was looking for, and they did a few sketches until I was happy with the design. When I got home, Isabel had dinner ready, and Lara was playing piano in the living room.

"Hi, popcorn," I said. I had given this pet name to Lara because she is so bubbly she reminds me of popcorn when it's getting ready.

"Jack, you're home." She ran to me, and I gave her a kiss on the cheek.

"I could hear you from my office, so I had to come home straight away," I said playfully. "No, you didn't. It's impossible to hear me playing that far, silly," she said very matter-

of-factly. Itmade me smile.

"Let's have dinner. Come on," I said, putting my bag down on the kitchen bench and going around the table, where Isabel was finishing setting the table. I kissed her.

"Had a good meeting?" she asked.

"No," I said, stifling a smile. I actually did have a good meeting, but it wasn't the meeting she was referring to.

"Oh?"

"The meeting was cancelled. They'll call in tomorrow to reschedule with you." "Okay. So is everything okay? You look happy. Something good happen?" "Something good happens every day since I've been with you," I said. God, Isounded corny.

"That sounded so corny," Isabel expressed my thought. We both laughed. I wanted to check about the marriage proposal thing, but I didn't know how to go on about it. Then I remembered that my dad's old secretary, Claire, was getting married, and I thought maybe I'd start with that.

"So Claire's wedding is when?"

"In March," she said as she dished out Lara's food. "Are you looking forward to her bachelorette party?" "I'm not going."

"Why?" I asked, curious.

"I'm not really the kind to go on those."

"What's wrong with bachelorette parties?" She gave me a look like *Really?* but I still didn't get why she didn't like them.

"First, drinking is not for me. Second, naked strippers rubbing on me? Yuck. And third, I'm always the one who has to carry the very drunk bride home, just to have her puke on me, so no more bachelorette parties for me, thank you very much."

Here was my opening.

"But you will have to go on your own bachelorette party one day, though," I said, not looking at her. I heard a big clang and looked up to see Isabel trying to clean up the mess she had just made. It seems she dropped the plateful of food onto the table.

"Oh, Mummy, you okay? Wait, I'll grab the kitchen roll." Isabel didn't look my way, but I knew she was blushing hard.

"Sweetheart, you okay there? Did I say something wrong?"

"*No*, no, of course not. You know me—I'm so clumsy, that's all." All right, maybe she wasn't ready for the proposal yet, but I'd try again just to be sure.

"Are you sure you're okay, or are you just not comfortable talking about marriage? I mean, I'm assuming you would one day like to remarry, right?"

She lifted her eyes to mine so fast, with such a shocked expression, trying to say something but clearly unable to, I could see then that she wasn't ready for this conversation.

"Hey, I don't mean right away. Maybe one day in the future." She instantly relaxed, and I deflated slightly. I was so ready to make her my wife, but she wasn't there yet. Of course she wasn't. I was so stupid. She had just said the words "I love you" not long ago. Of course she wasn't ready to get married.

Just cool it down, mate. Keep this good thing going, and soon she will be ready. You just need to be patient.

"Of course I would love get married one day—in the future." "What did you say, Mummy?"

"Nothing, honey, nothing at all," Isabel said, looking at me, pleading with her eyes to end this conversation, which, of course, I did.

CHAPTER 15

Isabel

I thought I was going to die when Jack was talking about marriage. Of course, since we got together, I have thought about getting married to him. We were living together, so the natural flow to the relationship would be getting married. And don't get me wrong; I think it will be the best day of my life when I hear him say "I do", but I wasn't ready yet. We were a couple now for eight months, and I loved the way we lived—our routine was so much like that of a married couple—but officially being someone's wife again frightened me. I wanted to be with Jack, and Lara sometimes asked me when were we getting married, but I believed that was more because my mother kept asking her if I ever mentioned marriage. My answer was always the same: "One day, baby. Oneday."

After that night, Jack never mentioned marriage again. I could see he was a little disappointed that night, but after that, it was as if he had never even mentioned it in the first place. To be honest, I have thought about it every day since. I can picture us marrying back home in Portugal, in the countryside, under a vine canopy on a wonderful summer's day, with lots of fresh flowers everywhere and our friends and family there to witness it. Unknowingly, I started to search the web for venues and dresses. This was stupid, though. I didn't want to get married now. Why was I wasting time looking for these things now? Why was I kidding myself? I did want to be Jack's wife. I wanted to be presented as Mrs Reed to everyone. I wanted him to call me his wife. But now I had made him believe I didn't, so I had to just put this behind me.

Oh, God, how I would love to have his baby, for Lara to have a little brother or sister to fuss over, Jack coming home and picking his baby up while Lara played a soothing piano tune and me watching them like a proud wife a mother.

Stop it, Isabel, just stop.

It was May, one year since we first met, when Jack called into the office just before I left.

"Do you need anything before I leave?" I asked, popping my head inside his office. "Come in. I have something you need to see," he said with a chirpy voice. I went over to his desk, and he came around it with something in his hand.

"I booked this a few months ago. I was considering telling you only a few days before flying, but I thought it wasn't wise. You might want to shop and probably prepare a few things, so ..."

He thrust his hand out, and there were tickets in them. When I looked closer, I realized he had booked a holiday for us—me, Lara, and my mum.

"I spoke to your mum, and she said you have a holiday home back in Portugal. She told me all the information I needed, so I booked the trip to Portugal, with activities for families so Lara will have plenty to do."

I do have a holiday home in Portugal, but I haven't been there since Sam died. It was too painful to go there. That house was a gift from my husband to me. He always said if he became successful, he would buy me a villa in Portugal and we would spend every minute we could in it. Lara was conceived there. I didn't know if it was a good idea to go back there with Jack. Jack must have seen my worry, because he tried to mend the situation.

"We don't have to go there if you don't want to. I was actually going to book us a house in the south of Portugal. I just thought to ask your mum, and she mentioned the house and that your family back home would be so happy to spend time with all of us. I can change it, though." He said all this in a rush. He kept cool though, and didn't show any nervousness. Jack was always in control— well, most of the time, that is—but I could see he had gone to all this trouble and was still trying to do what I wanted after all the work he done. He was so thoughtful that I couldn't deny himthis.

"It's okay. It's perfect, Jack," I whispered, looking into his eyes, my own eyes starting to tear up. I just wanted to let him have the last bit I was holding on to. I saw in his eyes that he was begging me to let him in, so I did. I let him know how I felt. I grabbed him and held onto him, crying softly.

"I still love him, Jack. I can never stop loving him. I'm sorry. I love you, but he still fills a space in my heart and always will. This house in Portugal was his gift to me. I need you to understand it is ours—Sam's and mine—and will always be. I hope you understand this. This will be the hardest I've done since Sam passed away, letting another man into the house. I even been there since he's been gone. I want to take you there, I want to stay there with you, but you need to be patient, and when we there, if I don't feel right, we have to leave. Can you do that?" I asked, looking at him again. I must have looked awful because I saw for the first time that Jack had tears in hiseyes.

"Isabel, I love you. I'll do whatever it takes. If you don't want to stay there, baby, we won't. I don't want to see this hurt. And yes, I understand you will always love Sam, and I'm okay with it. He was such a big part of your life, the father of your wonderful daughter. How can I ask you not to hold onto that piece of you? I'll arrange for alternative accommodations just in case. It will be there as a backup plan, okay?" he said, cleaning away my tears with his thumb.

God, what did I do to deserve this man? He had such a big heart, and I loved him so much. In that moment, I knew I wanted to spend the rest of my life with him. There was no one else more deserving of my heart than Jack, even though Sam was still there and would always be there. Jack occupied the majority of it now, though, and I gladly gave it to him.

"I love you, Jack." That was all I said. There was nothing else that mattered in that moment, just those simple words, but they meant more than anything else in the world. He smiled at me.

"Yeah, you've said that a few times lately." He kissed my lips and pulled me into his embrace, pouring out his feelings for me.

His hands were caressing both my cheeks, and his tongue was dancing with mine in perfect harmony.

I had three months to arrange a few things, like a deep clean of the villa and a temporary cook, which ended up being the cleaning lady who regularly cleaned the villa. She was great. I have known her since I was 14 years old. Her name was Clara. She was a local daughter of one of my mum's friends. The gardener was her husband, Francisco, who also did the maintenance of the property. Anything that needed doing, the two of them would do between them. When I called her and said we would be going over, she was so excited that by the end of the call she was in tears, which made my waterworks open too. The following weekends were spent doing shopping and preparing for the holiday. Lara was so happy. She never been to the villa. She had been to Portugal, as we went every year with my mum, but she had never stayed there. I will never forget Lara's face when we told her we were going to stay at the villa. She was so happy, and she started to tell Jack that she was "conserved" at the villa, which made both of us cringe and made her laugh at our reaction. She explained that my mum had told her that story many times.

"Can I load the car?" Jack asked from the entrance door.

"Yes, everything is here. I just need to get the portable cooler ready with snacks and drinks, so you can load the car while I do that," I said, feeling so happy and so ready for these holidays. Jack wanted to drive, but he didn't want to go the whole way, so he had help from Lizzy. He had booked the ferry from Portsmouth to Santander, in Spain, but that would be just me and him. Lara and my mum went by aeroplane; they flew out two days ago. As Lara was on her school and music holidays, she had more time than me and Jack, so when he said he had booked my mum and Lara to stay in Portugal for five weeks, with activities booked for both of them, I was both surprised and worried, but after speaking to my mum, she assured me they would be all right there together and that Lara wasn't a baby anymore. I had to let her stay with the family and get closer to her roots, she said, so I gave in. Jack and I had a deluxe suite on the ferry. I have been on the ferry before, but I never went so high end, so it was a first for me.

"Do you really need all this, Izy?" Jack asked. He had started to use the same pet name for me that Lizzy used, and I quite liked it.

"Yes," I said, smiling.

"Well, the good thing is that we're taking your car; otherwise, half this stuff would have to stay. Bloody hell, even after putting down the two back rows, the car is completely packed," Jack said, huffing and puffing as he came into the kitchen.

"Well, there is a lot we need when you have a child, you know?" "I'm starting to learn, yes," Jack said, chuckling.

"And Lara is big. When we have a baby, then you will understand why most people prefer not to go on holidays," I said, chuckling. He became really quiet, and I realized what I had just said. I closed my eyes briefly, and Jack came from behind me. He hug me around my middle section and whispered.

"Are you trying to tell me something?" His breath in my ear made all my hairs stand on end, as usual. I didn't know what to say, so I just shook my head slightly.

"But for us to have a baby without getting married first would be scandalous, you know, and we wouldn't want to be scandalous, would we?" he whispered. Again I couldn't talk. Oh, God, how much I wanted his baby, and how I wanted to be his wife. I just shook my head again slightly. "Good, so we agree not to be scandalous," he whispered, and he planted a small, sweet kiss on my cheek. To be honest, I was so distracted with the feeling and smell of him that I didn't understand his statement. He didn't wait for me ask anything. He just grabbed the cooler that I had prepared and took it to the car while whistling a happy tune. What justhappened?

Jack had a way of confusing me sometimes.

The trip was great. The ferry was more like a small cruise, and we had a twenty-four- hour journey. When we got off the ferry, after driving on the wrong side of the road twice, Jack finally agreed to let me drive. I couldn't stop laughing every time I looked his way.

"Stop it. I get it. I'm rubbish at driving on the wrong side of the road," he said grumpily. "It's the right side of the road here," I said.

"Well, it's stupid." I laughed harder, which made him laugh too.

A little later, Jack was staring at me with a goofy smile on his face.

"What? Do I have something on my face?" I started to rub my hand over my face gently. "No."

"So what then?" "Nothing."

"Well, it can't be nothing, looking at me with that funny face," I said, smiling.

"Can't I just look at my gorgeous girlfriend for no apparent reason other than her beauty?"

"Oh God, what are you planning? You have something planned, don't you? Dish. Come on. I know you, Mr Jack Reed Junior. You have something brewing—I can see it."

"What? No, I don't have anything planned." "Now I know for sure you do. God help me."

He just laughed

"I love you, Izy," he said, stroking my hair soothingly and leaning closer to me. "What're you doing? I'm driving, you know," I said, trying to concentrate on the road but finding it difficult with his touch and his breath now on my neck. "Can we just make a quick stop?" he whispered in my ear. "No ..."

Please stop, I thought. I could feel myself slowing down on the motorway.

"Please, I can't wait, I need you. Now," he said, breathing a little faster. He grabbed one of my hands and brought it to his hard shaft. Shit, it was so hard, like a steel pipe. I actually swerved slightly.

"Shit. Jack, stop it. We're going to crash."

"Well then, you have to stop before that happens, don't you?"

"Look, we have a petrol station coming up in a few miles. Just hold it until then." "Oh, baby, I don't know if I will be able to wait that long."

That made me chuckle.

"You will have to. Now, let's drive. The faster we get there, the faster you get what you want," I said, holding onto the steering wheel harder and putting my foot down on the accelerator.

"I'm sure it's not only what I want but what you want too." He started to rub at his shaft over his linen shorts, making little groaning sounds. Shit, it was making me so hot, so wet.

"Jack, I'm trying to concentrate here," I warned him. He didn't say anything. He just kept rubbing and groaning. The petrol station came into view, and I pulled up, parking closer to the toilets. I didn't wait or say anything. I jumped out of the car, and Jack followed, walking as quickly as I did. I pulled him into the men's toilets, locked the main door, and checked if anyone else was inside. Luckily, there was no one there, so I removed his shorts so fast it even took Jack by surprise. I pulled up my summer dress and grabbed his dick hard while he lifted up one of my legs. I didn't need any lubrication, as I was so wet that it went straight in. Jack and I groaned together. Jack grabbed me under my ass, and we both thrust into each other so fast, as if we had been starved for each other for years, not merely hours. It was rough and wild and just what we both needed. I came, and Jack wasn't far behind me. He said to me a while ago that when I come, it makes his dick go so crazy he can't hold back the urge to come too. Of course, it makes me come even harder just to know I do that to him.

We were still panting when a hard knock sounded on the toilet door and a Spanish man's voice came through, asking if everything was okay. I cleaned myself as quickly as possible and before unlocking the door I planted a kiss on Jack's lips. I unlocked the door and didn't look up to see the man standing in front of me. I just ran into the ladies' room, but before the toilet doors closed, I heard the man laughing and say to Jack in Spanish, "Well done." I was so embarrassed I didn't want to leave the toilet, but I had to. We still had a couple more hours of driving, and I wanted to get there as soon as possible, so I washed my hands and face for the third time and went out. Jack was leaning against the car, chatting with a couple.

"Oh, here she is," he said to the couple. "Hiya," I said with a little wave.

"Isabel, this is John and April. Guys, this is my girlfriend, Isabel."

"Hiya. So, you guys are going to Portugal. We are also driving to Portugal. We go there every year since we married."

"Isabel's family are from Portugal, so we are spending time with them." "Oh, *tu es Portuguesa?*" April asked me in Portuguese, which means "You're Portuguese?"

"No, I was born in England, but both my parents are Portuguese, so all my family is Portuguese. Your Portuguese is great, by the way."

"Thank you. I've learned by mixing myself as much as possible with locals while I'm there."

After a few more minutes of chatting, we drove off again. "You took your time in the toilets," Jack said with a little smirk.

"Well, I didn't want that man to look at me like I was a piece of meat, did I?"

"You mean you didn't want him to look at you and know exactly what we were doing in the men's toilet," he said playfully.

"Whatever," I said dismissively, although I was still embarrassed. "I think we need to stop in the next service stop too," Jack said. "Jack, stop it. God, you're insatiable." He just chuckled.

We were just around the corner, and I became really nervous. Everywhere I looked, the memories came crashing down. Jack noticed how quiet I was.

"You okay?" he asked as if he were speaking to a spooked animal. I couldn't muster any words, so I tightened my grip on the steering wheel and nodded. When the gates of the house came into view, I slammed on the brakes unintentionally. My breathing became laboured, and I felt every part of my body shaking. Jack grabbed my hand gently, drawing soothing circles on the top.

"Izy, we can go to the hotel, baby. We don't have to do this," he reassured me. I needed to do this, but the memories were like a flood out of control. I closed my eyes and focused on Jack's hand on mine. I leaned over to him and grabbed his neck, where I rested my forehead. I inhale deeply, filling myself with his strong scent, the scent which levelled my world, the scent that brings me back to him. I slowly opened my eyes and lifted my head, looking into those green clear bottomless river eyes of his, and all went calm.

My heart slowed, my breathing calmed, and I smiled, feeling as if he was the only thing that mattered at that moment.

"I love you, Jack," I whispered, and he smiled a kind smiled that I so much adored.

"And I you, Isabel," he responded with a little kiss on the tip of my nose. With that, I got the courage to press the button on my keys, and the electric gate opened. As the doors were wide open, Jack took a look at the house in front of him for the first time.

"Wow, Isabel, this is gorgeous," he whispered. We drove closer to the front door, and as I stopped, Francisco and Clara came out the front door. Clara didn't wait. She peeled my car door open and pulled me out, then embraced me tightly. We had been such close friends before Sam passed away. I didn't realized how starved of her closeness I'd been until now. I was crying so hard, holding onto her so tight, that I didn't realized Jack was drawing soothing circles on my back with hishand.

When I had finally stopped crying, Clara stepped back from the embrace and looked at Jack. With an appreciative look she whispered, "So, this is Jack. He's handsome."

I whispered back, "I know, right?"

"I can hear everything, you know," Jack said, smiling. "*Ola,* Clara. It's nice to meet you." He put his hand out and Clara looked at it quizzically.

"Oh my apologies. Two kisses, right?" he said, bending to Clara's level, which was far beneath him, and giving her two kisses, one on each cheek.

"Don't worry. You'll learn, *Senhor* Jack," she said in a thick Portuguese accent. "Oh, please, just call me Jack."

She smiled politely. "Come, I prepared a lovely dinner for you. You must be starving," she said.

"Be prepared with the amount of food there is. Portuguese people always cook for the whole village," I said to Jack under my breath.

"I hope you're joining us," I said to Clara. "Yes, Isabel, we'll join you."

I had forgotten how beautiful this place was, and I could see Jack thought so too. I breathed in the scent, so familiar, and smiled, thinking how happy I had been here with the man I loved. I only hoped I could be as happy with the man I now loved here, maybe make new memories. Jack hugged me closer to him with an unspoken question.

"I'm okay," I said simply.

"Go wash yourselves while I prepare the table, and Francisco will bring your bags up to you room. Isabel, I prepared the room in the right wing, as you requested."

"*Obrigada*, Clara."

When I opened the door, everything was the same but different. I couldn't explain. This wasn't my previous bedroom. I asked Clara to prepare this room for us because I couldn't go into the master room. In all honesty, this was a replica of the master, but the colours and décor were different. Where this was decorated in light blues and whites and had the feeling of the sea. My old room was decorated in greens and whites and had a feeling of nature, like being in a forest. I had decorated both myself, so I loved both.

"I'm just going to freshen up. Through here is the bathroom, and through there is the dressing room." I pointed so Jack knew the areas of the room.

"This is lovely, Izy. You do have great taste," he said as I entered the bathroom. "You know me. I love decorating," I shouted through the door. Jack chuckled.

When we finished dinner, I helped Clara clean up while Jack tried to have a conversation with Francisco, who spoke very little English. Clara and I kept laughing at their attempts to understand each other. I felt more relaxed now. It was great to have other people here. It helped my anxiety.

"He seems sweet and a good man, Isabel," Clara said in hushed tones.

"He is. He is perfect," I said, looking his way. He winked at me, making me smile.

"He clearly loves you, and you him. Anyone can see that, *querida* Isabel," she said, lifting my chin to look at her.

"We do love each other. I never thought I could love anyone other than Sam, but ... Jack has this way of getting into people's heart."

"Yes, he has. I spoken to your mama and Lara yesterday, and Lara couldn't stop talking about Jack. She loves him very much too."

I smiled again. "Yes, she does, and Jack adores her—which makes me love him even more." We both smiled.

"Well, I am so glad you finally found someone worthy of your heart, *querida*. Sam would be happy too, I'm sure." I nodded, unable to speak without choking.

Clara and Francisco left around 11 p.m. We were so tired. After taking a long, hot shower, we both went to bed, Jack holding me tightly to him.

"How you feeling?"

"I'm okay. It's difficult. I see him everywhere, but you're here with me, and I'm happy," I whispered, holding onto the arm he had around me a little tighter.

"If at any point you think this is too much, just say the word and we're off, okay?" he whispered back, planting small kisses on my ear and my hair. I simply nodded, already feeling sleep pulling me under. The last thing I heard was: "I love you, Isabel, more than anything in this world." And I was fast asleep.

In the morning, I stretched and felt the bed for Jack, but it was empty, so I got up and went looking for him. I heard voices from the kitchen, and when I rounded the corner, I saw Jack wearing shorts, riding low, and shirtless with a cup of coffee in one hand and a Portuguese pastry called *nata* in the other, laughing at what Clara was saying. When Jack spotted me, he put the pastry and coffee down and came to give me kiss.

"Hi, babe. I think I can get used to the food in here. Have you tried this pastry? It's amazing. Have a bit." He was so excited, it made me laugh.

"Yes, I have tried it. As amazing as it tastes, it puts every bit of that deliciousness on my ass," I said, smiling. When I looked at Clara, she wiggled her eyebrows and gave me a thumbs up from behind Jack. It was her way of saying he was hot. It made me laugh, and Jack looked at me as if I was going crazy.

"So, what is the plan for today?" I asked.

"Well, first we pick up Lara, and then we are heading to a place called Nazare—well that's the city name, actually. We are going to go to a water park. It's not as nice as the Algarve one, but apparently it's still fun."

"Right, I'll go get ready and pack for things for Lara too."

"Could you pack for me too?" he asked, giving me a sweet smile, trying to get his way (which worked, by the way).

"Okay, but if I miss your underwear don't, blame me," I said cheekily.

"I won't mind," he said just as cheekily.

When we went to get Lara from my uncle's house, she was so happy to see both Jack and me she just threw herself at us, and we all went in for a hug. <u>My family were so nice to Jack.</u> My uncle spoke only in Portuguese to him, and I had to translate the whole thing. Jack was a little embarrassed, but he tried to hide it. He did a good job, as only I noticed he was embarrassed.

"I need to take Portuguese lessons ASAP," he said when we got into the car. "Yes, you do, Jack, now that you ..."

She didn't finish her sentence, which made me look at her through the rear view mirror.

She was blushing and covering her mouth. Jack was looking out the window as if Lara hadn't said anything.

"This is so beautiful out here," Jack said while I was still mulling over what Lara had said, trying to finish the sentence. What did she mean? *Now that you are my mum's boyfriend?* If that <u>was</u> it, surely she would finish the sentence<u>, right?</u>

"Don't you think? Did you ever think one day you might move to Portugal?" he said, taking me out of my <u>own</u>thoughts.

"Oh, yes. It's beautiful, and no, I never thought about moving here. I love it here—don't get me wrong—but I couldn't leave England. It's my home."

"Oh, I don't know. Maybe when we are old and wrinkly and our children all <u>grown</u>up, I don't know ... <u>I guess</u>I could see us happy here in our old age," he said, smiling but still not looking at me. There it was again. He was talking about our future, presuming we would have children and grow old together. I didn't want to even think about it. It was too good to be true. If I let myself believe we would have that, I was afraid it would never happen.

"I guess … now that you put it like that, it wouldn't be too bad, not too bad at all," I said, trying not to smile.

"Oh, Mummy, and when I would visit you, you would make freshly-squeezed lemonade and we would sit by the beach. Oh, I want you to move here when you're old, Mummy." At that we all laughed. She says the funniest things, bless her.

The water park was okay. It wasn't amazing, but it was fun. We all ran around like children. I think Jack was more of a child than my own daughter. He kept pushing past us to always be the first to ride the biggest slide. Then he would do cannonballs, splashing everyone, which got him a few Portuguese swear words from other people. Then he would fill his water gun and splash us until it was empty, and then it would start all over again. God, I felt like I had two children with me, but it was an unforgettable day, just seeing Lara laughing so much and Jack's eyes sparkling as I had never seen them before. The only part I hated was the stares he got from every other woman in the park. Whether they were single or married, they didn't even hide it—they would gawk at him. Of course, he didn't even notice; he was too busy making sure I was always completely soaked. But I noticed, and when he would kiss me or hold me or smack my behind, their envious gaze made me a little better, because I had him. He was mine.

The days were passing too fast. One week had gone, and I was feeling so tired, probably more than when I was in England at work. When Jack said he had booked us activities, he wasn't joking. We did most water sports, climbing, trekking, site seeing—Jesus, I had never been so exhausted on a holiday. On the upside, I was now totally relaxed in my villa. I felt we all belonged there together.

"Babe, can we not do anything for rest of the week? I need to a rest," I groaned when I took my sandals off.

"Are you sure? There still so much we can do," he said, throwing himself onto the bed, clearly as tired as I was.

"Do you want me to dump your ass?" I said half-joking.

Jack laughed. "Okay, we'll take a break for two or three days, and if you change your mind, we can always get busy again. I need you to be fully recharged, anyway, for what I have planned."

Oh so he does have something planned. I knew it.

"Oh yeah, and what's that?" I said, fishing for information.

"You wait and see," he said with a sexy smirk. He jumped to his feet and went to take a shower, or so I thought. When he called to me and I entered the bathroom, there he was, inside the bathtub, with scented candles all around the bathroom and a Champagne glass in each hand.

"Come on, join me," he said, smiling that smile of his that always got my knees weak. I stripped slowly, letting him see I wasn't in a rush, then went back to the bedroom and put some music on my mobile. When I got into the bathtub, Jack gave me a Champagne glass.

"You know I don't drink," I said, but I took a lip anyway. "This is not alcohol," he said, smiling.

"I see what you're doing—trying to get me drunk again, are you?" I wiggled my eyebrows.

"God, you know me so well," he said, chuckling. I put the glass down and moved around, positioning my back to his chest. I wasn't surprised to feel his erection against my back. It seemed every time Jack looked at me he had a hard-on, which in turn turned me on. Just as badly. I laughed a little.

"How do you do that? It's like a light switch."

"Yes, a very hard light switch with a mind of its own," he said, laughing.

"With you it comes so easy, like the need to breathe." He whispered. He started to massage my breasts—not in a sexual way, but that made me even hornier.

"Yeah?" I whispered back.

We jumped at a loud knock on the bathroom door.

"Mummy, dinner is ready. Are you coming?" Lara was standing just on the other side of the door while we were fooling around.

This is so wrong.

"Yes, honey. We're going."

"Wait, is Jack in the bathroom too?"

Fuck, what was I supposed to say? She had never caught us in the bathroom together.

Shit. I jumped out of the bathtub while trying to dry myself with a towel.

"Well, yes, I just needed help with something, and you know Jack is so helpful." I covered my face, so embarrassed.

"Oh, okay. Don't be long. Grandma says she will start to eat without you if you take long."

"Okay." When we heard the bedroom door, shut we burst out laughing.

"Shit, that is the first time, and it better be the last time she catches us in the bathroom together," I scolded Jack.

"Okay, okay, I must admit, it was embarrassing."

When we got to the kitchen, everyone was looking at us. The first to speak was Clara. "So, everything okay?"

"Yes, why wouldn't it be?" I said quicker than I intended.

"Oh, I don't know. Did Jack help you with what you needed?" my mum said, smiling. "Yes, thank you for your concern."

"I bet he did help," Clara chipped in, and all hell broke loose. They were all laughing so hard, I felt my face was boiling. Lara just kept looking around, frowning.

"Why are you all laughing?" she kept asking.

"Oh, honey, nothing. They just had too much to drink. You see why you should ever drink alcohol, sweet pea. This is the reason." That made them laugh even harder.

"Poor Izy. You must be feeling so hot. Or maybe you're developing a fever. Your cheeks are so flushed," Jack said, making everyone laugh yet again. I gave him a murderous look. I felt I could kill him right then.

"Mummy, you're not feeling well? Jack is right, you seem too flushed," Lara said with concern.

"No, sweet pea. I'm okay. Just feeling hot—that's all," I said.

The food was fantastic, as usual, and as usual, I ate too much. Lately, I was eating so much more. It was like everything I saw, I needed to eat.

"God, I can't eat anymore. I feel like a whale," I said.

"You don't look like a whale. You are beautiful, sweet Izy," Jack said, kissing my lips sweetly.

"Ahem. There are children in the room," my mum said, smiling.

"Grandma, it's okay. I'm a big girl. I know when you have a boyfriend you kiss on the lips, and then, when you're married, you make babies," she said very matter-of-factly. We all stared at Lara. "What? We are starting to learn about this at school."

Okay I needed to know what she actually she knew, but not tonight. "I think I'll go rest. I feel so tired," I said, yawning.

"Me too. I'm beat," Jack said, rubbing his eyes.

"Mummy, can I stay up a little longer? I can help Clara tidy up and then go to bed." "Clara, would you put her to bed for me?" I asked.

"Sure. Don't worry. You go on, and I'll sort this little lady out." "Good night, everyone?" both Jack and I said at the same time.

We were so tired that we didn't have any sex. We just lay in bed, and I was out in seconds. In the morning, I put my bikini on and went to the pool. Jack was still asleep—bless him. He tried to keep us busy exploring, doing all sorts of things, and now that he knew we wouldn't go anywhere, he was dead to the world. It was after twelve when he came to find me.

"Hi, beautiful," he said, bending down and kissing me.

"Hey, I was getting worried you weren't going to wake up." He lay down on the chair next to mine.

"I was completely beat. I feel tired still," he said, closing his eyes, letting the sun inside his pores.

"I can see that. Are you coming down with something, you think?" I asked, a little concerned.

"No, I don't think so. I think it's all just catching up with me." "Oh, poor baby," I said playfully. He chuckled and looked at me.

"I love you, Isabel." He said it so serious, it made my heart miss a bit. Why was he so serious?

"I have a surprise for you tonight. Your mum is staying in your uncle's house with Lara, and tomorrow they are all going to the beach, so I planned something relaxing for us here at the house—if that's okay with you."

"Of course it is. I'm up for anything relaxing."

"Great, so, at 2 p.m., we're having a massage with two great masseuses—so Clara tells me—then we are having dinner outside in the garden. How does that sound?" he said, coming closer to me.

"It sounds divine," I whispered back, smiling. When I thought Jack would kiss me, he picked me up and threw me into the pool.

"*Jack* ... fuck ... I could drown," I shouted at him, trying not to laugh but failing. "I would never let you drown." Then the kiss came.

The massages were great. I felt renewed. My muscles didn't ache anymore, and I felt beautiful at the moment in my long, loose red silk dress and with a golden tan I loved.

"You ready, honey?" Jack asked from behind. He had been gone for about an hour, saying he needed to do a few things, asking me not to leave bedroom until he came for me. I looked at him, and, God, I was gawking. He looked gorgeous, so delicious, that I wanted to eat him right now. He was wearing smart navy blue linen trousers, a white slim fit shirt with the buttons opened halfway down, letting me see his perfect chest, and a pair of summer shoes. He was glowing as well. This weather was so good we were both glowing.

"Yes, can you tell me now what you were doing?" I asked, excited.

"In a little bit, you will see." He grabbed my hand and pulled out of the bedroom. When we were near the bifold doors in the living area, he turned to me and said, "Close your eyes for me, Izy." I did as he asked, and he guided me out. Then he stop and said, "You can open them now." What I saw made me gasp. There were dozens of twinkling lights in the garden, candles around the swimming pool, and two huge vases, one on each side of a single round table filled with red and white roses. The table was laid beautifully, with a bottle of very expensive looking Champagne in an ice bucket to one side of the table. Everything looked beautiful, and I was surprised that all this took him only an hour.

"Francisco helped me, and the local florist came to help with the flowers and candles too," he said, anticipating my unsaid question.

"This is … this is amazing, Jack." I grabbed his shirt and kissed him.

"You're welcome, my sweet Izy." He pulled my chair, just like the gentleman he was, and took a seat opposite me. Clara and Francisco served us, and before leaving, Clara told Jack dessert was in the fridge. He just needed to grab it, as it was ready. When dinner was over, Jack seemed a littlenervous.

"You okay? You look worried. Did anything happen?"

"No, I'm okay. Everything's okay," he said, dismissing my worry with a little wave.

"I'll be right back." He got up and went inside. He was behaving strangely. Every time he looked at me, he had a goofy smile, as if he was smiling at something only he understood. He also kept looking at my hands and kissing them. I knew I was being paranoid, but he had been acting stranger than usual.

Soft music started playing. While I waited for Jack to come back, I listened to the song— "Perfect" by Ed Sheeran. It made me smile. Jack came out with one single rose. He gave it to me and grabbed my hand.

"Dance with me, beautiful." I took his hand and we started to dance to the music. "I chose this song because the lyrics are exactly what I think of you, my love," he whispered. Some people might think this was corny, but me … I thought this was complete heaven. Here I was, dancing with a gorgeous, thoughtful, sweet, caring, loving, successful, intelligent man who had just dedicated a beautiful song to me. What could be better than this? God is real, and he just gave me an angel.

The song ended, and another started—Calum Scott and Leona Lewis's "You Are the Reason". He had such a good taste in romantic music. We carried on dancing a little bit more, and then Jack pressed a little remote in his hand that I hadn't noticed before, and everything went dark apart from the candles surrounding the swimming pool. Jack turned me around, placing my back to his chest, and I realized the candles weren't the only thing on. There was a single line of twinkling lights forming two words, two words I had to read over and over. When I turned back to him, he was in one knee with a little red box in his hand. It was open, displaying the most beautiful engagement ring I had ever seen. There was a beautiful pearl in the middle, surrounded by small diamonds. The diamonds went to the sides as well. The shine it gave off was mesmerizing. He remembered how much I love pearls.

"Isabel de Sousa, since the very first moment I accidentally crashed into you, my world brightened. You showed me what real love was. I didn't fall in love only with you but with your wonderful daughter. I want to spend the rest of my days making both of you happy. Would you make me the happiest man in the world and marry me?"

He looked into my eyes so intensely and with such certainty, I knew he meant every word he said. If he had asked me three months ago, I would have said no, but now ... there was only one answer.

"Yes," I choked out. Tears of happiness spilt out from my eyes, and Jack jumped to his feet, lifting me up and kissing me as though he needed my kiss to survive. When he realized he hadn't yet put the ring on my finger, he put me down.

"Sorry, baby. Here, let me." When the ring was on my finger, he kissed it, closing his eyes.

"Today is the happiest day of my life. Thank you," he said, grabbing my face with both his hands and looking into my eyes. He kissed me passionately, and I him. The kiss soon turned hot, and before I realized it, I was already taking his clothes off. He just took both my thin straps of my dress, and it fell onto the floor. I was wearing a red strapless one-piece teddy.

"God, Izy, what did I do to deserve you," Jack said while kissing my neck, then my shoulder. He opened the back of lingerie, and it too fell to the floor. I was now naked in the garden while he was in his boxer shorts. I took control a little, and he let me, looking at me with such hunger it made my insides clench instantly. I kissed his chest and slowly went to my knees and kissed his firm abs. The closer I got to his hard shaft, the harder he moaned. I finally took him into my mouth, grabbing his shaft with my hand, working it from a slow rhythm to a faster one. I kept flicking my tongue on his head, and I could see he wouldn't last long if I carried on this way, so when he pulled me up, kissing my neck and grabbing my ass, I circled my legs around him. He walked over to the living room and laid us on the sofa. In a slow thrust, he entered me. It was so good, the feeling of him being inside me, filling me with his thick dick. I couldn't think of a better sensation. He was made for me. I moaned so loud when I climaxed. Jack exited from me before he could come. Then he turned me around and onto my knees, on the floor. He started to play with my asshole, like he did often, but this time he was dragging some of my juices from my sex to the hole, massaging it and fingering me. It felt so good. As he played with the asshole he started to play with my clit too, and I was soon panting, close to the edge again. He didn't stop. Instead, he increased the tempo. I hadn't noticed his dick digging into my ass until he was pressing hard and the head was inside. I screamed a little, but I didn't know whether it was pain or pleasure, because I climaxed just as Jack entered me completely. He groaned hard.

"Fuck, baby, this is so tight. Shit, it feels so good."

He started to thrust a little bit faster now that he saw I was enjoying it too. I never in a million years thought I would do anal, but here I was, and actually enjoying it quite a bit too. He was careful, and I knew he wanted to go harder, but he didn't. He took his time, slowly, so I could adjust to him. He wet the fingers of one hand and flicked my nipples while the other was playing with my clit. God, he was so good at this. I found myself trusting into him faster, close to another climax.

"Oh, Jack. Harder ... faster," I moaned. "Fuck me like you want to," I shouted. He growled and started to thrust harder and faster, until we both climaxed. It came so hard that my tummy hurt from the strong spasms that came over me.

We were lying on the large fluffy rug in the living room, still panting. I propped myself on one arm, looking at him—his lips, his eyes I always get lost in, his soft light brown hair, his flushed cheeks. He was perfection, and he was all mine.

"You were the first," I said, looking into those beautiful green eyes of his. He understood what I meant right away. He smiled and caressed my face with a thumb.

"Thank you, baby, for everything you've given me. I know how hard it is for you to let go, and I'm honoured that you chose me—to give all of yourself to me and to let go of the past too. You don't know how important it is to me," he whispered.

How I loved him. I thought it would be impossible to love again, let alone to love this much. I kissed him slowly and then lay on his chest. I barely remember Jack lifting me into his arms and carrying me into the bedroom in the middle of the night, but when I woke up looking into those gorgeous green eyes staring back at me, his lips on my hand, which was wearing the ring he had put there last night, I could only smile the happiest smile I never had.

"Good morning, beautiful," he whispered.

"Good morning, gorgeous." He smiled too, not taking away his gaze, even for a second. I could live like this forever, waking every day in his arms, looking to those eyes and losing myself in them.

What am I saying? I agreed to all those things last night, when I said yes. Now he was mine, and he will always be, just as I imagined.

We had such a lazy day, lounging around the pool, having crazy sex. Jack binding me was becoming a habit and something I truly enjoyed. It intensified my senses. Everything became more sensual and pleasurable. In the evening, we decided to go for a walk in the beach. It was a fifteen-minute drive, which was nice. The cool breeze coming through the open windows in the car was so soothing. Jack was driving now, as we had been here for over a week and he had gotten used to "the wrong side of the road", as he called it. The night was clear, with the bright moon shining and the busy city night on one side while on the other, the waves crashed with a calming sound.

"I love the sound of the sea," I said. "It's so soothing, isn't it?"

"How will we tell Lara about us getting engaged?" I asked. This had been nagging me all day.

"Ah, so that's what's been on your mind." He smiled, hugging me closer. I just nodded my agreement. "You don't have to worry about that. Everyone knew I was proposing. They haven't heard anything from us, so I'm pretty sure they all know you've said yes by now."

I looked at him, shocked.

"Wait, what? How did they know you were proposing? Okay, Clara and Francisco—I knew that they knew, but the others?"

"Well, I asked your mother for your hand, and then I asked Lara for both your hand and hers. She didn't hesitate—she said yes right away and said your answer would be the same.

Your mum, Lara, and Lizzy have known for about a month now."

"What? A whole month and not even Lara cracked?" I was so surprised. "Well, Lara almost did—in the car, if you remember, on our first day out."

Oh yeah, her unfinished sentence. Now it all made sense—all the hushed conversations between Jack and Lara and the small giggles every time I entered a room. Now it all fit into place. How couldn't I have seen it?

"You are so sneaky—and getting everyone else in it too," I said playfully.

"I wanted everything to be perfect, including the timing. I needed to make sure you were ready. I never wanted to rush you or make you uncomfortable. I needed all the people you love to help me with it, and it worked." He chuckled a little.

"Yes, it did, and I'm pleased you did it how and when you did it. I'm ready to be your wife, to have a family with you and build a great future together."

"Good, because I don't know what I would do if you weren't ready for all that. I need you like I need air to breathe. Yeah, I know I sound corny, *again*, but it's true, and I don't care if I do sound corny. It's who I am and what I feel for you." We both laughed.

We left the beach and started to walk along the sidewalk. I noticed some guy with a grey hooded top coming our way. He was looking at me, but I couldn't see his face. The hood threw a shadow across his face. A sense of dread came over, me and I stopped in my tracks. The figure continued approaching us, and I grabbed Jacktighter.

"What is it, Izy? You okay?" Jack asked, looking at me. I couldn't take my gaze away from the figure, coming closer, at a slow pace. The first thing I noticed was his eyes, his kind, dark eyes.

No, Isabel, you're making all this up in your head.

When he passed by me and looked into my eyes everything slowed at that moment. All I could see were his eyes—his sad, hurt eyes. Jack was next to me, trying to get my attention, but I let go of his hand and turned away from him, towards the man who ... I knew it was impossible

... I grabbed his arm and shouted his name. "Sam?"

When he turned, there he was, staring at me—afraid, unsure, and sad so, so very sad. Sam my supposedly dead husband, was there standing in front of me, not dead at all. All I saw next was a black void. My heart felt so tight. The last thing I felt was an embrace, an embrace that just moments ago felt right, warm, home. It was now cold and numb.

To be continued ...

ABOUT THE AUTHOR

I was born in Portugal on 8 April 1986, and moved to Leamington Spa, England, in 2001, when I was only 15 years old. I studied business in college and married at 18 years old while studying, and I had my first son when I was 25 years old. I got divorced at 28 years of age and met my present husband straight after. I moved to Northwood, London, where my husband had his Landscape business, in 2014. I had a little girl in October 2016 and got married in August 2017, in Portugal. I have two children of my own and a stepson who spends a few days a week with us. I have always been very creative, with lots of stories to tell, and I am a bookaholic. The only thing that helps me to relax is a good book.

ABOUT THE BOOK

Isabel is widow of four years, previously married to famous tennis Sam Winter, who died in a plane crash over the Atlantic while returning from a tournament in Spain. Isabel never dated in all that time, until she met Jack, who crashed into Isabel's car. Their attraction was instant; however, Isabel thought she would never see him again. The day after the accident, at a board meeting, he was presented to the board members and their PAs as the company's new CEO. Wanting to get Jack out of her head, she started to date William, a university professor.

However, the attraction between Isabel and Jack continued to grow, and Jack would do anything to get Isabel. However, things would not come easily for the pair, as ghosts from both of their past would reappear to challenge their love.

www.ingramcontent.com/pod-product-compliance
Lightning Source LLC
Chambersburg PA
CBHW071931190726
48293CB00004B/1231